KAT WOLFE
ON THIN ICE

BY LAUREN ST JOHN

Wolfe and Lamb Mysteries

Kat Wolfe Investigates
Kat Wolfe Takes the Case
Kat Wolfe on Thin Ice

Legend of the Animal Healer Series

The White Giraffe
Dolphin Song
The Last Leopard
The Elephant's Tale
Operation Rhino

Laura Marlin Mysteries

Dead Man's Cove
Kidnap in the Caribbean
Kentucky Thriller
Rendezvous in Russia
The Secret of Supernatural Creek

One Dollar Horse Series

The One Dollar Horse
Race the Wind
Fire Storm

Stand-Alone Novels

The Snow Angel
The Glory

Lauren St John

KAT WOLFE ON THIN ICE

Farrar Straus Giroux
New York

Farrar Straus Giroux Books for Young Readers
An imprint of Macmillan Publishing Group, LLC
120 Broadway, New York, NY 10271

First published in Great Britain by Macmillan Children's Books, 2021
Printed in the United States of America by LSC Communications US
Designed by Aurora Parlagreco
First edition, 2021

1   3   5   7   9   10   8   6   4   2

mackids.com

Library of Congress Cataloging-in-Publication Data

Names: St John, Lauren, 1966–, author.
Title: Kat Wolfe on thin ice / Lauren St John.
Description: First edition. | New York : Farrar Straus Giroux Books for
Young Readers, 2021. | Series: Wolfe & Lamb mysteries ; book 3 |
Audience: Ages 8–12. | Audience: Grades 4–6. | Summary: Stranded alone
while vacationing in the Adirondacks, twelve-year-old best friends
Kat Wolfe and Harper Lamb leave their snug cabin to search for a
missing witness in a criminal case, while a blizzard nears.
Identifiers: LCCN 2020025364 | ISBN 9780374309640 (hardcover)
Subjects: CYAC: Mystery and detective stories. | Robbers and outlaws—Fiction. |
Missing children—Fiction. | Blizzards—Fiction. | Best friends—Fiction. |
Friendship—Fiction. | Adirondack Mountains (N.Y.)—Fiction.
Classification: LCC PZ7.S77435 Kav 2021 | DDC [Fic]—dc23
LC record available at https://lccn.loc.gov/2020025364

Our books may be purchased in bulk for promotional, educational, or
business use. Please contact your local bookseller or Macmillan Corporate
and Premium Sales Department at (800) 221-7945, ext. 5442, or by email at
MacmillanSpecialMarkets@macmillan.com.

CONTENTS

KAT WOLFE ON THIN ICE

For Ruth Wilson,
with love and heartfelt thanks for reminding me,
when I needed it most, why stories matter

SPY CRAFT

THE SLOWER THE TRAFFIC MOVED, THE faster Kat Wolfe's heart beat.

Thud-thud it went, as brake lights flared and the speedometer jerked from seventy miles per hour to zero.

Thud-thud-thud as the taxi driver turned up the radio, which announced that a spill of oranges was causing long delays on the motorway up ahead.

Thud-thud-thud-thud as the minutes ticked by and the pained sighs of the driver and tense breaths of Kat and her mum, Dr. Ellen Wolfe, and Harper and her dad, Professor Theo Lamb, steamed up the windows.

"I don't mean to sound like a stuck record," said Dr. Wolfe, "but are you girls absolutely sure you have your passports?"

Harper plucked hers from a pocket. Kat searched her rucksack with increasing desperation. She was ready to declare a national emergency by the time Harper discovered it wedged between the seats.

"What are best friends for?" said Harper with a grin.

It was barely 11:00 A.M., but already Kat's heart had endured more palpitations than a high-wire walker's in a gale.

At dawn, it had spiked when her alarm shocked her awake. Though it was still dark and rain pummeled the windows of her attic room in Bluebell Bay on England's Jurassic Coast, she'd squealed with excitement.

In just seven and a half hours, she and her veterinary surgeon mother, who seldom took a break and deserved one more than anybody Kat knew, would be escaping the dullest, drizzliest October ever and taking an actual proper holiday.

Better still, they were going on vacation with Harper and her dad to the United States, the Lambs' home country.

Best of all, they'd be spending eight days in New York.

"Oh, Kat, what I'd give to be in your shoes," veterinary nurse Tina Chung had said dreamily as Kat bolted a bowl of Choco Krispies. "Breakfast at Tiffany's, the bright lights of Broadway, the glamour and glitz of Fifth Avenue, the Metropolitan Museum—you'll be doing it all. Hopefully you'll also get a chance to twirl through the autumn leaves in Central Park."

"Fall," Kat told her. "Harper says that in the U.S.

autumn is mostly known as 'fall.' And I don't think we'll have time for any of those things. Except for twirling through the leaves. There'll be plenty of leaves in the wilderness."

"Sure, there are wild bits in Central Park, but I'm not aware of any—"

"Not *Central* Park, although we might catch a glimpse of it when we stop over in New York City on our way back. For the first week we're going to the *Adirondack* Park in upstate New York. It's about a five-hour drive from the city. A friend of Professor Lamb's has loaned him a cabin in the wilderness. Apparently, there are bears. Bobcats too! And moose! I can't wait."

Catching sight of the clock, Kat flung down her spoon and dashed off to finish packing.

Twelve trips up and down the stairs in search of lost gloves, a missing pajama top, and the mystery she'd saved to read on the plane had sent her heart rate rocketing again. But what really pushed it into the red was trying to find Tiny, her not-so-tiny, half-wild Savannah cat. He'd gone off in a sulk as soon as the suitcases appeared.

"I can't leave without saying goodbye to him, I just can't," cried Kat as her mum shepherded her up the garden path. The taxi was waiting, engine snarling.

"You can and you will if you don't want to make us late for our flight," said Dr. Wolfe. "It's a three-hour journey to London's Heathrow airport, and that's only if

3

the traffic is kind to us. Anyway, you've already said the longest goodbye to Tiny in history. You know very well that Tina will take excellent care of him."

"Don't worry, Kat," the nurse reassured her. "I promise to feed Tiny world-class fish dinners and play mouse-toy games with him every single day."

"Hear that, Kat?" said Dr. Wolfe. "World-class treats and mouse-toy games. Five-star cat-sitting, he'll be getting. Now you can relax."

And with that, she'd more or less shoved Kat into the cab.

Of course, like most parents, Ellen Wolfe was a great deal better at dishing out advice than taking it. When her phone rang as she was sliding onto the back seat, her daughter shrieked, "DON'T ANSWER IT!"

"I have to." Dr. Wolfe leaped out of the car as if the seat had caught fire. "It might be an emergency."

"That's exactly why we've arranged for a locum to help me look after your patients while you're gone—to deal with emergencies," chastised Tina. "He'll be here within the hour."

"Yes, but what if it's urgent?" The vet dug her phone out of her pocket. "Bluebell Bay Animal Clinic, Ellen Wolfe speaking. How may I help you?"

Twenty-five minutes later, the Wolfes and the exasperated taxi driver were finally on their way, leaving behind one patched-up Jack Russell and one beaming

4

owner. Kat was smiling too because she'd found Tiny hiding in the wardrobe and had been able to give him an extra-special cuddle before leaving.

"Travel safe. Stay out of trouble!" Nurse Tina called, as the driver revved the engine like he was on the starting grid of the Monaco Grand Prix.

"We're going on holiday—there won't *be* any trouble!" Kat yelled out of the window as they zoomed away.

"There will be if there's a holdup on the motorway," grumbled the driver. "Your holiday will be delayed, then."

"That's why we've allowed tons of extra time—so we'd have wiggle room if anything went wrong," Dr. Wolfe informed him sweetly. "Turn left at the junction. We have to make a quick stop to collect our friends."

There was nothing quick about it. Professor Lamb, a paleontologist, was on the phone dealing with a dinosaur inquiry. Kat and Harper took advantage of the delay to run down to the field to give farewell kisses to Charming Outlaw, their shared horse.

Eventually, the taxi left Bluebell Bay. The driver radiated disapproval at their tardiness, predicting fog, flat tires, and other catastrophes up ahead.

"It'll be gridlocked around Winchester—don't say I didn't warn you . . .

"You'll wish you'd left earlier if we hit roadworks near Basingstoke . . ."

When he could bear it no longer, Professor Lamb said, "Sir, thanks for your concern, but I'd appreciate it if you'd let *us* do the worrying."

For one hundred kilometers, they flew along without a care. Vacation spirit filled the car. Dr. Wolfe and Professor Lamb sang country songs at the top of their lungs. Kat and Harper bantered about the terminal uncoolness of parents and made thrilling plans.

Each tried to decide which part of the trip they were most looking forward to.

For Kat, it was the animals. She thought she might die of happiness if she saw a real bear.

Harper couldn't wait to show Kat the maple trees in their fall finery and introduce her to American buttermilk pancakes. British pancakes were never the same.

Dr. Wolfe pictured herself hiking up mountains by day and drinking cocoa beside a crackling log fire at night.

It was as Professor Lamb talked dreamily of the hawks he hoped to capture with his new telephoto lens that the taxi came to a screeching halt.

Ahead, one thousand red brake lights pulsed angrily.

"What did I tell you!" declared the driver. "It's always best to leave early. Catastrophe lurks around every corner."

His passengers sat in glum silence, watching the clock.

"We'll be fine," said Dr. Wolfe, gripping the door handle with white knuckles. "If this jam clears soon, we'll easily make our flight."

"Yes, we will," seconded Professor Lamb. "We only have six miles to go and half an hour to do them in. Think positive, kids."

Two highway patrol cars screamed past, nearly giving Kat a heart attack.

The radio crackled. A traffic reporter boomed: "We regret to announce that police are closing the southbound M25 in order to clear an overturned lorry and five tons of squashed oranges. Or should that be orange squash, ha, ha! Expect long delays."

"No!" gasped Dr. Wolfe. "We'll miss our plane!"

Harper was outraged. "How can they do that? There are ambulances carrying sick patients, and families going on vacation."

"This is *my* fault for delaying everyone at Paradise House," said Professor Lamb.

"No, no, it's mine for seeing a nonemergency patient before we set off," insisted Dr. Wolfe. "I'm sorry, girls. I've ruined everything."

"No, you haven't," Harper told her. "Me and Kat wasted time too."

Kat wanted to cry. Not just because she'd been looking forward to seeing the bears for months but because her mother was so crushed and exhausted.

Putting her patients first yet again might have cost her the holiday she desperately needed. It didn't seem fair.

"There must be *something* we can do," said Harper. "We're so close. If only we had a hot-air balloon to whisk us over the fields to the airport."

Kat's heart began to race. Harper's words had given her an idea.

With everyone distracted, she messaged her grandfather.

SOSOS!!!

Her phone lit up.

Did you mean SOS? Are you in deadly danger again, Katarina?

No, but it's sort of an emergency. We have 20 minutes to get to the airport or our holiday is toast. Don't spose you're nearby & can work a miracle?

Nearby, yes. Unfortunately, helicopters can't land on a busy highway.

We're parked beside an empty field!

Hmm, tricky, but not impossible. En route to
London Heliport but will change course directly.
Expect me in eight mins. Be ready & waiting.

How will you find us?

Do you really need to ask?

Kat burst out laughing. If the United Kingdom's minister of defense couldn't locate his own granddaughter, he wouldn't be much use at fighting spies or stopping wars.

"Mum! Harper! Professor Lamb! Everyone out on the roadside with your luggage. The Dark Lord's on his way."

No one would believe her at first, but Lord Dirk Hamilton-Crosse, aka the Dark Lord, was as good as his word. He came flying to their rescue in his own private chopper: a sleek flying machine so futuristic that Harper had nicknamed it the "Spy Craft."

The Spy Craft freed them from their traffic prison with ease, levitating above the snarl. It whirled them to Heathrow's private general aviation terminal at record speed. The cabdriver watched them go, mouth agape.

They'd been whisked to the gate in moments by a limousine.

"One minute later and we'd have closed the flight." The woman at the check-in smiled.

"Quick, let's have everyone's passports," she said, holding out her hand.

Professor Lamb rifled through his camera bag once, twice, three times. The color drained from his face. "Harper, everyone, I'm so sorry. I forgot mine."

Harper giggled. "Dad, stop kidding around. The whole way here, Dr. Wolfe kept asking me and Kat if we had ours."

"Did she? I must have been miles away, thinking about dinosaurs or hawks. What a boneheaded, peanut-brained dingbat I am."

He hugged his tearful daughter tight. "I feel terrible, but thankfully, this is easily fixed. I'll hop on the next train back to Bluebell Bay, grab my passport, and catch the first available flight to New York. You'll hardly have time to miss me."

Kat's heart was still hammering as she buckled up her seat belt, and not just because they'd had to sprint for the plane. Before they'd even crossed the Atlantic, trouble had found them.

Before they'd even crossed the Atlantic, they were one man down.

SLEEPLESS IN THE SLEEPY-TIME INN

HARPER TOSSED, TURNED, AND TOSSED some more. The bed linen was scratchy, the pillow crackled in her ear, and the room was stuffy and airless. She felt like a Thanksgiving turkey being broiled alive. She wondered if her dad had had a sleepless night too. He'd be kicking himself for making such a silly mistake, feeling guilty for letting her down.

You'll hardly have time to miss me, he'd told her. But Harper missed him now. Each time she shut her eyes she saw him fading into the distance at the airport, shoulders slumped as he prepared to take a series of slow trains back to Bluebell Bay.

She sat up and put on her sneakers.

"Where are you going?" Kat asked from the other bed. Her mum was in the next room, soft snores drifting through the connecting door.

"To get some OJ from the drinks station in the lobby. Wanna come?"

"Definitely."

Kat couldn't sleep either. Too much sugar. On the flight over, the vegan meal had resembled astronaut rations. To stave off starvation, she'd munched her way through an entire bag of Candy Kittens. Her mum didn't say a word. Following the debacle with Theo Lamb's passport, she'd gone overboard trying to compensate for his absence and make Harper feel better.

"*Of course* you can watch another film," she'd said when the credits rolled on the first. "Here, have some caramel popcorn. There are Skittles in my bag too if you're peckish. Yes, you can have more soda."

She'd dozed off soon afterward, leaving the girls to watch back-to-back movies and eat junk. By the time Kat emerged, dazed, from the entertainment-fest, they were coming into land at Newark airport. Flipping up the blind, she'd pressed her face to the cold window.

The Boeing 747 bumped through a gloom of cloud, tipped a wing, and burst into the light. Kat sucked in a breath. The legendary New York skyline was on fire. The setting sun had turned the skyscrapers into towers of molten gold.

She'd had a bird's-eye view of the Statue of Liberty, torch held high above the glittering bay, before the plane thudded down. As it sped along the runway, the cranes loading the shipping containers on Newark Bay resembled golden giraffes leaning down to drink.

Getting through passport control and collecting their bags and the Chevrolet Traverse that the professor's friend had kindly loaned them, had taken forever. The small and quirky Sleepy-Time Inn was only a short distance away, tucked just off the highway, but it was after midnight U.K. time when they were finally settled into their rooms. Kat had been shattered. She had no memory of getting into bed.

Now it was 5:50 A.M. Kat was buzzing. It was her first visit to the United States. She did not want to miss a thing.

"We're the same, you and I," laughed Brenda, the receptionist, watching Harper put a splash of orange juice in a glass and top it up with crushed ice from the ice machine. "I like OJ with my ice too!"

Kat filled hers up with juice alone. "I don't understand. It's the crack of dawn and chilly outside. Why do you need ice?"

Harper grinned. "Because ice is nice!" She crunched up a mouthful appreciatively.

"Millions agree," said Brenda.

She gestured at the reception sofa. "Take a seat if you like. You girls hungry? It'll be a while till the kitchen staff lays out the continental buffet. Want me to toast you a couple of cinnamon-and-raisin bagels while you wait for your mom to surface?"

"Yes, please!" Kat didn't think her mother would mind. Brenda had been on duty when they'd arrived. She'd been so welcoming and helpful when they were exhausted. Besides, Dr. Wolfe's room was only three doors along the corridor.

"Okay if I turn on the news?" asked the receptionist as she brought over two warm, plump bagels and a choice of spreads. "This side of the pond, we're transfixed by the Wish List gang drama. The law caught up with them last week. One of them anyway. They say he's the ringleader. He appeared in court last night, but this is the first chance I've had to watch it."

"The Wish List gang?" Harper spread cream cheese thickly on her bagel. "Never heard of them. What's with the weird name? Is it some bucket list thing?"

"Good guess, but not exactly. They're master thieves. Over the last couple of years, they've pulled off a string of outrageous heists. Art, rare books, unique antiques—you name it, they've stolen it. They're like ghosts. Different cities. Different targets. The only link between them was a list left at the scene of each crime."

"A wish list?"

"You got it," said Brenda. "Nine items, written real simple, like a kid's letter to Santa—if Santa were a billionaire. Number one: a priceless painting. Number two: a Ming vase, and so on. Not that a kid would want a Ming vase, but you get the picture."

Kat's bagel lay untouched. "How did the police catch up with them? What happened?"

"Same thing that always happens, hon. They got greedy and got caught. Least this one did. Cops are hoping he's going to rat on the others."

A red banner scrolled across the television screen. ALLEGED WISH LIST GANGSTER DENIES THEFT OF $50 MILLION NECKLACE.

Brenda turned up the volume. "There he is now: King Rat. This is only the arraignment, mind you—a pretrial hearing. The real trial won't happen for a couple of years."

A figure with a coat draped over his head was being helped from a prison van. The watching crowd surged forward, and he stumbled on the courthouse steps. Guards helped him up, virtually carrying him the rest of the way.

Inside the courthouse, he was assisted into the dock. As the guards stepped back, Brenda gave an incredulous laugh: "*That's* the ringleader? Let me guess—his other accomplices are a dozen red-nosed reindeer."

Kat giggled. "He does look a bit like an arthritic Father Christmas."

"Maybe he is," joked Harper, "except he kept the best gifts for himself."

But all three stopped smiling when the defendant spoke in a low, querulous voice to confirm his name and age: Gerry Thomas Meeks, ninety-one. He gave his address as Shady Oaks Nursing Home, New Jersey. His face was creased with laughter lines, as if he'd once been jolly. Now it was haggard, and he tugged nervously at his white beard.

"How do you plead, Mr. Meeks?" asked the magistrate judge.

"Not guilty, Your Honor."

The prosecutor snorted in disbelief.

The judge banged her gavel. "Any more of that and I'll hold you in contempt, Mr. Talan. And while we're on the subject, I hope you have a watertight case. Life is short, and so is my temper."

"Your Honor, we have a star witness who will prove beyond doubt that Gerry Meeks is a criminal mastermind who snatched the diamond necklace at the Royal Manhattan Hotel while security guards helped tackle a blaze across the street."

The prisoner looked more dejected than ever. As he was led away by guards, a tall woman with a sweep of dark hair whispered something to him.

"That's Rachel Scott," Brenda told Kat and Harper. "She's a big-shot defense attorney. Heaven knows why she's representing Gerry Meeks and why she's doing it pro bono. That means no win, no fee."

Reporters clamored around the lawyers as they emerged from the courthouse.

"Who are Mr. Meeks's accomplices?"

"Will he name them?"

"Will he reveal where he's hidden the diamond necklace?"

"Who's the star witness?"

Rachel Scott paused, crimson coat swinging. "Ladies and gentlemen, this is a clear case of mistaken identity. Mr. Meeks is a blameless senior who struggles to climb five steps. You saw that with your own eyes. The idea that he could mastermind a string of heists the length and breadth of the United States beggars belief."

"Save the speech, Rachel," snapped Kasper Talan. "If he was so innocent, the judge wouldn't have denied him bail. No, far from being a decrepit ninety-one-year-old with amnesia and bad knees, Gerry Meeks is as cunning as a fox. A resident at Shady Oaks recalls him winning at chess and doing yoga in his room. That's how smart and limber he is.

"Our star witness will reveal how Gerry Meeks slipped the jewels into his coat pocket, the very same pocket where detectives later found a copy of the wish list. He was so sure he'd get away with his crime that he'd had the audacity to check off number nine on the list: a diamond necklace."

"And where is that necklace now?" asked Rachel,

cool as snow. "Do you have it? Do the cops have it? Oh, it's still missing, is it? As I suspected, bungling detectives plan on scapegoating an innocent old man to cover up their own incompetence."

She turned with a cheery wave. "See you in court, Kasper T."

The news clip cut to a grinning TV anchor. "There you have it, folks. A wily fox or a blameless senior? Ringleader of the Wish List gang or a heartbreaking case of mistaken identity? We'll keep you posted. In other news, New England residents batten down the hatches for ninety-mile-per-hour winds and possible snow as back-to-back weather systems, including a strong nor'easter, are set to arrive on—"

Brenda muted him. "Whaddya think, girls? Guilty or innocent?"

Kat glanced at Harper. "We believe that people are innocent until proven guilty."

"But if you had to guess?"

"Innocent," said Kat.

"Guilty," said Harper.

Brenda nodded. "I'm with you, Harper. I'm not buying the sweet-old-grandpa act for a second. Nobody steals a fifty-million-dollar necklace unless they're as sharp as a steak knife. Wonder where he's stashed it."

Kat didn't answer. She was staring at the screen. A weather forecast graphic showed a shape-shifting fireball spitting icy arrows as it barreled toward the northeast coast of the United States. "What *is* that?"

"What's what, hon? Oh, they're predicting Snowmaggedon for New England. A polar vortex is sweeping south from Canada. Something to do with a low-pressure system tugging freezing air from the Arctic. But don't worry. Up north in the Adirondacks, it's going to be a perfect day."

RUBY RAIN

"OH, I DO LOVE A ROAD TRIP," SAID Dr. Wolfe as the highway hummed beneath their wheels. "There's something so romantic about heading into the great unknown, especially when that unknown is a million-acre wilderness park. And we couldn't have asked for more glorious weather."

"If only Dad was with us," Harper said wistfully. "Thank goodness he's found his passport, so he should be here tomorrow or the day after."

Kat was only half listening. Nose pressed to the window, she watched road signs flash by on Interstate 87, pointing the way to New York City, Albany, Saratoga, Troy, and—beyond the Adirondacks—Montreal, Canada.

Everything was new and yet somehow familiar, as if she were in a Hollywood film come to life. A red barn against a bright blue sky. A black truck with monster tires and two dogs leaning out, tongues lolling. A milkshake drive-through. Lorries that Harper called semis carrying bread, eggs, and corn. Holstein dairy cows ambling home.

Lining the highway were trees in shades of rust and green-yellow.

"Are those the legendary fall colors?" asked Kat, who was less than impressed. Harper had told her that tourists came from across the globe on "leaf" holidays. To come so far and be met with trees that were no better than the ones in Bluebell Bay was a little disappointing.

"Be patient!" teased Harper. "Wait till we get to the Adirondacks."

Patience was not one of Kat's virtues. Not unless it involved animals, in which case she had all the patience in the world. Restless and fidgeting in the back seat, she willed the Chevrolet to do a quantum leap to the distant forest.

For eleven years, Kat and her mum had lived in a cramped, fume-filled part of London, the streets noisy with honking, drilling, hammering, and bursts of music and arguing. It wasn't until she moved to Bluebell Bay that she realized she needed nature the way she needed oxygen. The farther she got from cities, the better she liked it.

Which was why her spirits had soared when Harper and her dad had invited the Wolfes to join them for a log cabin vacation in the wild heart of the Adirondack Park. Harper had grown up in the neighboring state of Connecticut, where her father had been a professor at Yale University. Now she had few connections to her hometown, so she hadn't minded when her dad suggested they spend fall break in the Adirondack wilderness. He'd spent many happy summers there as a boy.

For months, Kat had thought of little but Nightingale Lodge, which the cabin's owner, Ross Ryan, described as a "haven of tranquility on the edge of a lake." Even the park's name, which she'd had difficulty getting her tongue around, conjured up images of campfires and shy deer peeking between pines: *Ad-i-ron-dack*.

"It comes from a Native American term *ha-de-ron-dah*, meaning 'bark-eater,'" explained Harper. "That's what the Iroquois tribe used to call their rivals, the Algonquin. They didn't think much of their hunting and berry-gathering skills. The Iroquois and Algonquin were the first people of the Adirondacks back when it was one of the toughest places on earth to survive. The winters were long and brutal. Often there was still snow on the ground into May. The summers could be a nightmare too. The woods were crawling with hungry bears and bugs. Rattlesnakes too."

"Gosh, you're really selling it to me," Kat said wryly.

Harper rolled her eyes. "Nowadays there's heating and bug spray, and people know they need to lock down any food if they don't want their cabin doors clawed off their hinges or their tents ripped open by scavenging bears. *We* have it easy."

Not everyone had it easy, Kat discovered, when they stopped for a rest break at the Inquiring Minds Bookstore in Saugerties, a quaint town in the Catskills. Cross-legged on the floor of the travel section, she pored over *At the Mercy of the Mountains: True Stories of Survival and Tragedy in New York's Adirondacks.*

"*Your brain is your biggest asset . . .*," advised the author. "Those people that remain calm, don't panic, and then logically reason out their situation are the ones who most often survive."

The cover showed a man signaling for help in a snowbound landscape.

The sparkles in the snow reminded Kat of the diamond necklace. What would a ninety-one-year-old in a nursing home want with $50 million worth of jewels?

Then again, why would a real thief plant the wish list on a "blameless senior"? It didn't add up.

"Good choice," said a voice. "Forewarned is forearmed."

Kat jumped guiltily, as though she were the one with the wish list in her pocket. A mother cradling a sleeping baby and a copy of *The Very Hungry Caterpillar* was smiling at her and nodding at the book.

Kat put it down. "Umm, er, have you visited the park?"

The woman laughed. "I used to live there, so more times than there are lakes and ponds in the Adirondacks. There are close to three thousand of those. That's not counting the thirty thousand miles of streams and brooks feeding twelve hundred rivers. And don't get me started on the number of mountain ranges and wild animals. There are four thousand bears alone."

"Wow. That's a lot of wilderness."

"Sure is. Three steps off the trail in the wrong direction can turn a stroll in the woods into a major search-and-rescue mission. Blink and a person's gone. Now you see them; now you don't."

Kat resolved never to stray so much as a millimeter from any trail. "How do the rescue crews find them?"

"First, they try to pinpoint where they were when they vanished. That's often the trickiest part. Those tasked with naming six million acres' worth of ponds, peaks, roads, and rivers ran out of inspiration early on. For every Lake Tear of the Clouds or Train Wreck Point, there are nine Deer Creeks, two Mirror Lakes, and thirteen Bear Roads. When friends say, 'Jack said something about hiking near Bear Road—dunno which one,' that's not real helpful."

"We've been hunting everywhere for you, Kat," said Dr. Wolfe, rounding the shelves with Harper and three mugs of hot chocolate. "There are so many nooks and crannies in this glorious store that one literally could get lost in a book."

The woman smiled. "I do that all the time. More fun than getting lost in the woods."

Harper hooked her arm around Kat's. "Come on, let's go. The leaves are calling!"

Kat hung back long enough to say to the woman with the baby, "Nice chatting to you."

"You too. Enjoy the beautiful Adirondacks. They say that once you've breathed the High Peaks' air and felt the ruby rain on your skin, you'll be forever changed."

CALL OF THE WILD

AFTER EVERYTHING SHE'D READ AND heard, Kat expected to feel the earth shift on its axis when they crossed the border of Adirondack Park, but it wasn't like that at all. Lake George, the first town they came to, was just as neat and picture-perfect as Bluebell Bay.

Granted, she had never seen a stag sharpening its antlers on a mailbox before, but her seaside home had its fair share of exotic creatures. Seals and dolphins, for starters.

And, Kat thought with a shudder, spies. Her early days as Bluebell Bay's first pet sitter had not worked out the way she thought they might. Not at all. If she hadn't met Harper and accidentally formed a detective agency, Wolfe & Lamb Incorporated, she wasn't sure she'd have survived them.

Judging by its tame appearance, Lake George was pleasingly spy-free, but Kat had learned the hard way that appearances could be deceptive. Perfect places often hid perfect crimes. If jewel thieves lurked in nursing homes, any crime was possible anywhere.

"What's ruby rain?" she asked Harper as the golf courses, burger joints, and water parks slipped away behind them.

"You'll know it when you see it" was her friend's enigmatic reply.

Kat was travel weary and fed up with waiting and seeing, but before she could say so, the sunlight caught a maple tree, transforming it into a living flame.

Her breath caught in her throat. While she'd been lost in thought, suburbia had given way to forests with wildfire colors. White birch trees were crowned with gold, and groves of beech and oak with flaming orange.

As the road twisted higher, the first crags poked above the trees. Red maples ablaze with hues of crimson, fuchsia, and vermilion turned every mountainside into nature's most spectacular art gallery.

"*Now* do you see about the leaves?" Harper asked with a smile.

Awed, Kat could only nod.

Wildness came into the car like smoke. It was in the clean, sharp air, in the secret silver inlets, and in the talons of the rough-legged hawk that swooped past their windshield to snatch a bloody scrap of roadkill from the asphalt.

Dr. Wolfe stamped on the brakes to avoid it. Barred feathers strained in its wings as it powered away, amber eyes gleaming with triumph.

They stopped for a late lunch in Ticonderoga, a tiny hamlet with the atmosphere of a frontier town in a Western. As they parked beside the lake, two trucks and a Harley-Davidson biker sped off, loaded up with firewood, bottled water, and provisions.

"Wonder what's going on," said Dr. Wolfe. "It's as if they're preparing for a siege."

Hardly had she spoken when the door of the general store slammed with a jangle and the open sign flipped to shut. A bundle of newspapers was marooned outside. One headline caught the girls' eye. TOP SECRET WITNESS HOLDS KEY TO WISH LIST CASE.

"Must be someone mega famous," mused Harper.

"Or royal," suggested Kat.

The proprietor of the Full-Belly Deli was on a ladder, boarding up the windows.

"Any chance of a meal?" asked Dr. Wolfe.

"Soup and crackers is the best I can do. We're shutting early today on account of the weather."

"The weather? But there's not a cloud in the sky."

The chef slid down the ladder and exchanged his hammer for an apron and ladle. "Around here, that can change in a heartbeat. Since yesterday the birds have been acting strange. Not singing; leaving in flocks. The woodsmen are predicting a nor'easter storm the likes of which we haven't seen in years. Blizzards and gales. The whole kit and caboodle."

"That's not what the weather app is forecasting," said Dr. Wolfe, smiling.

He gave her a hard stare. "When it comes to the weather, I'd trust an Adirondack local over the app on my phone any day."

Seeing their disbelieving faces, he warmed to his theme inside the dimly lit diner. Halloween pumpkins lined the windows.

"You ain't experienced winter till you've lived through winter in the Adirondacks. At home, we have a rope stretching from the house to the barn, like the early settlers did. Least we know we ain't gonna die of exposure if we get lost in a snowstorm tending to the horses."

Harper was skeptical. "Lost in your own backyard? But never in October, right?"

"You'd better believe it can happen in October."

The sun was still shining when they drove away with bellies full of delicious tomato soup, three blankets—"just in case"—and a sketch directing them to the best leaf-viewing road through the backwoods.

"It's pretty as a picture, but don't linger," warned

the chef. "You wanna be tucked up in your cabin by nightfall."

They had every intention of being in their cabin by nightfall, but it was near impossible not to linger. The track was a pale ribbon of dirt winding through the flame-leaved forests, empty apart from the occasional hiker or lone vehicle.

Each turning they took was more breathtaking than the last. Dr. Wolfe and Harper kept hopping out of the car to take photos. Kat took the opportunity to peer between the pines, hoping to spot deer or moose.

She was curious too about the human forest dwellers. They were few and far between. She'd seen some idyllic log cabins in sunlit glades and others with moss-covered rocking chairs on the porch and rusting cars in the yard.

Now, though, there was only forest.

"How much longer till we reach our cabin?" she asked plaintively as they stopped for yet more leaf pictures. "I need the bathroom."

Her mum sighed. "Why didn't you go when we stopped at the gas station?"

"Didn't need it then. Now I do."

They were in luck. Around the very next bend was a nature-viewing area, with an arrow indicating a compost toilet in the woods.

The cubicle was occupied. As Kat sat on a fallen tree to wait, an SUV grumbled into the parking lot.

Through the foliage, she watched a tall man, a stocky woman, and a girl of about her own age get out of the vehicle. On the road, a police squad car rolled by.

"Goodness, it's like Piccadilly Circus in the wilderness," said Dr. Wolfe. "Kat, Harper and I will be right over there taking photos of the lake. You'll be able to see us. Yell if you spot a bobcat on the prowl. We'll come running."

She and Harper headed down to the water's edge with their cameras, comparing notes on film and shutter speeds.

Shortly afterward, the woman and girl came up the path, the former saying peevishly, "I asked if you needed the restroom when we were at the gas station and you were adamant you didn't."

"Well, now I do. You shouldn't have given me chocolate milk."

"I was *trying* to keep you hydrated."

The woman seemed taken aback to see Kat sitting on the log. "Oh, hey there."

Her gaze darted from Kat to the closed door of the cubicle to Dr. Wolfe, who chose that moment to wave to Kat from the lakeshore. Relaxing, the woman smiled warmly at the girl. "Sweetheart, I need to make a call.

I'll be under that shelter at the trailhead. Holler if you need me."

The girl perched on the log beside Kat. She was wearing a cherry-pink baseball cap and a cornflower-blue neckerchief the same color as her eyes. "Always in trouble," she said with a conspiratorial grin. "Why can't they understand that when you don't need it, you don't need it, and when you gotta go, you gotta go!"

"Don't worry, I just had the exact same conversation with my mum," said Kat.

The girl's father materialized near the shelter. He had a buzz cut and arms as thick as maple branches. His aviator glasses glinted briefly in Kat's direction. As he leaned against a post to talk to the woman, his voice carried clearly through the trees. "Who's our girl talking to?"

"Some kid."

"Yeah, but what if—?"

"Quit fussing. We're in the middle of nowhere."

"Why's she chatting? We need to get going."

"There's a line."

"A line? Out here—in the middle of nowhere?"

"I guess there's a shortage of restrooms in the wilderness."

The man snorted with laughter. "Well, there's no shortage of trees."

"Yeah, but every tree trunk might conceal a sleeping bear."

"You think there are bears in these woods? *Grizzlies?*"

"Black bears. Four thousand of 'em."

"You're kidding? Four *thousand*? Uh, I think I forgot to lock the vehicle. I'll go check on it."

Kat did her best to pretend that she hadn't heard, but a giggle escaped as she pictured the man hunkered down in the vehicle, hiding from invisible bears. She clapped a hand to her mouth. "Sorry, I didn't mean to laugh at your dad."

The girl laughed. "No offense taken. He's not my dad anyway; he's my uncle. Personally, I'd love to see a grizzly or any other bear. I *adore* animals."

"Me too." Kat smiled. "Especially cats. I have one. A Savannah. He's quite wild and so enormous that the man who rescued him called him Tiny as a joke. Want to see him?" She slid a photo out of the sleeve of her phone.

The girl studied the picture with delight. "That's hilarious. Tiny, your own personal leopard. I'd do anything for a cat like that. At home in New York City, I'm not allowed any pets. My dad claims he's allergic, but I don't believe him."

A long desolate cry cut through the trees from the lake. Kat jumped up. "What *was* that?"

"Only my favorite sound in the world. It's a male

loon's yodel. They're divers—aquatic birds—with black-and-white plumage. They always look as if they're dressed for the Oscars."

She cupped her hands and mimicked the loon's haunting call. To Kat's astonishment, the unseen loon responded.

"My nan taught me that," the girl said proudly. "She's crazy about birds. Dad thinks she's crazy in every way, but that's only because she's as fierce as a lioness when it comes to righting wrongs."

A shadow crossed her face. "Last time I saw her she was, anyway . . . Uh, do you think we should knock? Whoever's in the restroom must be taking a nap."

Kat was beginning to suspect that the cubicle was empty but was reluctant to say so because she was intrigued by her companion. "Let's give it another minute. Tell me more about your nan."

The girl brightened. "She's tough and cool and doesn't care what anyone thinks. It freaks Dad out that she's dyed her hair every color of the rainbow. A lot of people talk about helping others or saving nature. She goes out and does it. One time she found out that the reason the loons on a lake near her house were being careless parents and forgetting to feed their chicks was because this evil company had leaked toxic metal into the water. They were the sorriest people on earth by the time she got through taking them to court."

The woman was calling from the path. "Riley, sweetie! Everything okay?"

"All good . . . Aunt Jo. Still waiting."

As her aunt moved away, Riley lowered her voice. "Can I let you in on a secret? I don't actually need the restroom. It was an excuse to be in the woods for a while, breathing in the pines. I used to come here a lot to see my nan, and I miss it. These trees, the loons, they're like friends to me, and I don't have many of those. Not real ones."

Impulsively, Kat said, "This is my first time in the Adirondacks, and I don't know where anything is, but if you're staying anywhere near us, maybe we could hang out sometime this week. I mean—if you wanted. Sounds as if you love animals and nature as much as me and my best friend, Harper, do. We'll be your friends in a heartbeat. I'm Kat with a *K*, and that girl taking photos of the leaves is Harper."

The girl gave her a strange look. "I wish . . ."

Out of nowhere came a furious, icy whirlwind. It tore through the high branches and churned up old leaves and twigs, sending gold leaves cascading over their boots. Whitecaps stampeded across the lake. Then, just as abruptly, the wind was gone.

In the silence that followed, scarlet maple leaves floated down. Kat fancied she could hear their jewel-like tinkle. They landed soft as velvet on her upturned cheeks.

"Ruby rain," she breathed.

Riley gave a joyous shout. "Yes, ruby rain!" She twirled around like a ballerina en pointe.

Kat blinked. Riley's uncle was crunching at speed through the debris, as inscrutable as a commando in his aviator shades. He smiled at them in a way that made Kat think he was not in the habit of smiling.

"Apologies for interrupting, ladies, but time is marching on. Riley, have you forgotten your cousins are preparing a meal for us? It might be speedier for you to use the restroom there. Say goodbye and let's go."

He strode off up the path, clearly expecting her to follow.

Riley's smile was gone. "Bye, Kat with a *K*," she said politely. "Good to meet you. Hope you have a good vacation." She hurried after her uncle.

"Wait!" Kat ran after her and pressed the photo of Tiny into her hand. "I want you to have this. He looks scary, but he's the best friend anyone could ever have. He's my protector, and I'm sure he wouldn't mind being yours."

The girl was momentarily speechless. "B-but I don't have anything to offer you in return. No, hold on, I do. Have my BUFF neckerchief. It'll keep you warm. Winter weather's moving in. That whirlwind was a warning."

"Then *you'll* need it," protested Kat, but Riley rushed away and didn't look back.

"Kat, Kat, check out these photos," cried Harper. "The shafts of light turn the forest into a cathedral."

As Kat admired the images on Harper's camera, she sneaked a glance at the tree-lined parking lot. It was empty apart from their car. Faster than seemed possible, the family in the SUV had gone.

Now you see them; now you don't.

CAR TROUBLE

"KAT, WOULD YOU MIND TAKING ANOTHER look at the map?" said Dr. Wolfe. "If I'd known the phone signal in these parts was so nonexistent, I'd have brought the GPS from my own car. It would have been comforting to have it, especially with night closing in."

Harper fervently agreed. The sky had turned the color of a bruised plum. The clouds were swollen with dark intent. Crosswinds played tug-of-war with the car. The chef at the Full-Belly Deli had been right. A nor'easter was moving in.

Kat wrestled once more with a map that took up the whole of the back seat. "Got it! We're on Mohawk Road heading west."

Harper twisted around. "That can't be right or we'd be halfway up a mountain. Also, we're heading north. Let me have a go at finding it."

"I'll pull over," said Dr. Wolfe, trying to ignore the orange warning light that kept flickering on the dashboard. "We'll search for it together."'

She parked on the shoulder and switched off the engine. "Harper, pass me Ross Ryan's directions to the cabin. Hmm, they seem straightforward enough: 'Take the second left after mile marker twelve on the A road to Blue Mountain Lake. Proceed slowly along Otter Creek Road to Mirror Lake. After you cross Deadwood Bridge, the road forks. You can't miss the sign for Nightingale Lodge. There are no near neighbors. True isolation! Happy holidays!'"

Kat's phone suddenly blinked into life. So, for a minute, did Google Maps. "Good news! We're on the A road to Blue Mountain Lake."

"And there's mile marker nine right there." Harper lowered the window to point. Icy air gusted in with enough force to shake the car. Hastily, she shut it out. "Only five miles to our cabin."

Dr. Wolfe laughed with relief. "Oh, thank goodness. For a moment, I was a little worried."

She turned the key in the ignition. Nothing happened.

She tried again.

And again.

"Why won't it start?" Harper asked anxiously.

Dr. Wolfe dug out the manual for the Chevrolet and

started paging through it. "Could be the alternator . . . or the battery . . . or the starter. Whichever, we need a mechanic. Unhelpfully, my phone hasn't worked since I dropped it at the hotel this morning. Kat, do you still have a signal?"

Kat did. What she couldn't do was reach the operator at All-Star Roadside Assistance, the company used by Ross Ryan.

"You are . . . eleventh . . . in line," said the recorded message. "Due to a high volume of callouts, our valued customers may have to wait longer for help. Thank you for your patience and understanding . . . You are . . . eleventh . . . in line . . . Due to a high volume . . ."

While Kat held on for a human, her mum used Harper's phone to dial the caretaker at Nightingale Lodge.

Annette Brody answered on the first ring. The signal was weak and intermittent. Dr. Wolfe put the call on speakerphone as they all strained to hear.

"You poor, poor things," said Mrs. Brody when she learned they might be hours late. "What a welcome to the Adirondacks, and what a shame to arrive just as we belatedly learn that a winter storm is on the way . . . Tell you what, why don't you send . . . food . . . warmth . . . fire . . ."

"Excuse me?" puzzled Dr. Wolfe.

"My . . . jet will be coming your way . . . thirty minutes . . . toddler twins . . ."

"I'm sorry, I didn't catch that. Did you say your jet is on its way?"

Gales of distorted laughter issued from the speaker. "If only! I said my nephew Jet will be driving your way in about thirty minutes . . . Twin girls . . . Truck with a tow bar. Give you a ride to the local gas station . . . Wait for help in safety and warmth."

"Bless you," said Dr. Wolfe. "However, I'm not sure what time the roadside assistance people will show up . . ."

"That's why I'm suggesting you send the girls on ahead to Nightingale Lodge. Jet can drop them off. Give him the directions . . . Never been here . . . I'll be at the cabin till . . ."

The connection went down, redialing several times.

When it reconnected, Mrs. Brody was in full flow. "Refrigerator full of food, a crackling fire, books, and games . . . join them as soon as your vehicle's fixed."

"You're too kind," said Dr. Wolfe. "If you're sure we won't be imposing on Jet, that would be tremendous, especially if nasty weather is moving in. Knowing that the girls are safely in the cabin while I deal with the car would be a huge weight off my mind."

A NARROW ESCAPE

KAT WATCHED THE GAS STATION'S NEON sign recede into the twilight. It felt wrong, leaving her mum behind. Not because Dr. Wolfe wasn't in good hands or because Jet and his three-year-old twins weren't lovely, but because in less than forty-eight hours their party of four had halved.

"Go ahead and eat dinner when you get to the cabin," her mum had instructed the girls. She'd kept Kat's phone in case of emergencies and would contact Harper with any updates. "Hopefully, the car will be easy to repair and I'll join you for dessert."

Jet slowed the truck and swung onto Otter Creek Road. "Harper, from here on, I'll need Ross Ryan's directions."

For the first time since entering the Adirondacks, Kat felt a strong sense of unease. The forests they'd driven through earlier had been peaceful sanctuaries of glorious color. Now they were in true wilderness: secretive and fraught with peril. Black treetops thrashed overhead, straining in the wind. The steep and rocky road was littered with pine cones and twigs.

Night bore down on them like a juggernaut.

"I'm hungry," Avery said sorrowfully.

"I want to go *home*," demanded her twin, Olivia.

"Soon as we've taken Ms. Wolfe and Ms. Lamb to their house, we'll go to ours," their dad said soothingly.

"Are you a wolf?" Olivia asked Kat.

"You don't *look* like a wolf," accused Avery, tugging at Kat's tangled red-brown hair.

"It's not what's on the outside that counts, it's what's in your heart," said Harper, who was sandwiched in the back between their luggage and the twins. "Kat's as brave as a tiger and as loyal as a wolf."

Kat grinned. "Right back at ya, Harper Lamb."

"If you're a lamb, why are you friends with a wolf?" Olivia asked Harper.

"Because she's the nicest wolf anywhere," Harper assured her.

Everyone laughed. Kat was glad of the distraction. Through the trees, she'd glimpsed a silver Airstream trailer, its ramshackle yard walled with NO TRESPASSING and THESE DOGS BITE FIRST & ASK QUESTIONS LATER signs.

Above the trailer door was a further warning, framed by two painted guns: IF YOU'RE FOUND HERE TONIGHT, YOU'LL BE FOUND HERE IN THE MORNING.

Kat shivered. Who else and what else lived in these woods?

"If there are thousands of bears, how come we haven't seen any?" she asked Jet.

"They're out there—you can count on it. Thing about wild animals, they always appear when you're least expecting it."

"Hope so!"

"Don't be fooled into thinking that black bears are cute and cuddly," cautioned Jet. "Never, ever go for a walk without bear spray."

"Bear spray?"

"There'll be some in your cabin. Used wisely, it'll save you. Don't go using it till the bear is within twenty-five feet, else you'll really make it mad."

They rattled across Deadwood Bridge. A creek hissed below.

"When a bear's on the *a-t-t-a-c-k*," Jet said, spelling out the word so as not to scare the twins, "every instinct will *s-c-r-e-a-m* at you to sprint for your life. Resist it. Your life depends on you doing the opposite. Stand tall, cling together, and make plenty of noise. Back away very, very slowly."

"Look! Nightingale Lodge!" Harper broke in excitedly.

They'd reached the fork in the road. A signpost was twisting in the wind. It was, as Ross Ryan had told them, unmissable. A cartoon nightingale pointed the way.

"Nearly there," Jet said with relief.

They crested a rise and had a split-second vista of Mirror Lake before the road dipped and the forest screened it out. Jet bumped downhill for another five minutes before braking at a gate signposted: PRIVATE. KEEP OUT.

"I don't see my aunt's vehicle in the driveway. Let me check if she's messaged me." Frowning, he fished his phone out of his pocket.

"Oh, that makes sense. She's prepped the property and headed home to miss the worst of the storm. We must have just missed her when we turned off the main road. Says here she's sent a text to your mom, Kat. Will you girls be okay for an hour or two till Dr. Wolfe gets here? I should really get the twins home."

Harper glanced surreptitiously at her phone. Unsurprisingly, Mrs. Brody's text had gone to her by mistake. The caretaker had assumed that Dr. Wolfe had used her own phone when she'd rung earlier. She'd simply hit redial.

The girls' eyes met in silent agreement.

"We'll be absolutely fine," Harper told Jet.

"Totally," seconded Kat.

"Awesome. I'll get this gate open and settle you into your cabin before I leave."

As he climbed out, the wind seized the door and almost wrenched it from its hinges. Freezing air blasted into the truck, drawing shrieks from the twins.

With difficulty, Jet wrestled aside the gate. He clambered back behind the wheel and slammed the door. "Hope your mom gets here soon, Kat. It's shaping up to be a wild night."

He put the truck into gear and was rolling forward when there was a crack like a rifle shot somewhere above them. Jet jumped on the brake. An oak branch crashed down, missing the truck by millimeters. A split second later and it would have smashed through their windshield.

The twins burst into wails of terror. Jet leaned over the seat to soothe them, reaching for their small hands. "All right, all right, Daddy's got you. The big, bad wind huffed and puffed and blew the tree down, but don't be scared. Nothing's gonna hurt you in my truck."

"Jet, you should just go ahead and take Avery and Olivia home," said Harper, pretending a confidence she didn't feel. "We can let ourselves in, no problem."

"Thanks, Harper, but I promised Dr. Wolfe I'd see you safely to the door."

The branch was blocking the driveway. It was

immovable, so Jet jumped out of the truck to help carry the girls' bags to the cabin.

"Daddy, don't leave us!" Olivia sobbed hysterically.

"Where's *Mommy*?" screamed Avery.

"Honestly, Jet, we can manage," said Kat. "Why don't you wait here with Avery and Oliva until you see us go inside? That way, you'll know we're safe before you leave."

Jet didn't have much choice. The twins were inconsolable.

The front of the cabin was on stilts, overlooking the lake. The porch light for the side entrance was on. Harper had the code for the key safe, but there was no need for it. The door was unlocked.

They waved goodbye to Jet.

He tooted in response before doing a U-turn. Yellow headlights strobed between the trees as the truck swept up the hill and out of sight.

There were no other houses. No near neighbors.

The girls picked up their bags and let themselves in.

NIGHTINGALE LODGE

KAT HAD A PICTURE IN HER HEAD OF A dream wilderness cabin, and Nightingale Lodge ticked every box. The animal art alone made it perfection. Even the doormat made them laugh: DOGS WELCOME (PEOPLE TOLERATED).

Above the stone fireplace was an oil painting of wolf pups playing in the snow. Every lamp on every table was a bear sculpture. Bathed in a soft glow, bears guzzled trout, climbed trees, or nuzzled their cubs.

For obvious reasons, Annette Brody hadn't left a roaring furnace unattended, but the wood and tinder were well prepared. One match and the fire crackled into life, turning the cold living room into a fragrant, cozy home in minutes.

The furniture was rustic but comfortable. There were two squashy sofas, a rocking chair, and an armchair large enough to sleep in. There was also a spotless, well-stocked kitchen, a breakfast bar, and a dining table.

The top floor of the A-frame log cabin consisted of a shower, a landing crammed with books, and a twin bedroom, where the girls dumped their bags. Like the larger bedroom on the lower ground floor, it faced the dark hill behind. Kat pushed up the blind but could see nothing but moving shadows.

Back in the living room, Kat and Harper stood side by side staring out of the floor-to-ceiling window. The racing clouds cleared at intervals and a bright moon strobed through. On a sunny day, the view would have been spectacular. Still, something inside Kat thrilled at the sight of Mirror Lake whipped by the wind into a turbulent silver sea. The jagged silhouettes of violently swaying trees obscured its outer edges.

There were no stars and only a few pinpricks of light on the far side of the lake, on the lower slopes of a black mountain. As the girls looked out, icy pellets began to pelt the glass. Purple clouds blacked out the view.

"It's as if aliens have abducted everyone and we're the only people left in the world," said Kat, only half joking.

"Luckily, we have a whole army of bear sculptures and a life-sized toy raccoon to keep us company," said Harper. "Books too! And a refrigerator packed with food!"

Kat grinned. "It's kind of fun being on our own in

the wilderness. If my mum wasn't arriving shortly, we could have played music at full blast, stayed up till two A.M. reading, or had a midnight feast."

"Not sure if I could have waited for any midnight feast," said Harper with a laugh. "I'm starving. How about we investigate what Mrs. Brody's left us for dinner?"

Annette Brody hadn't written them a note, presumably because she'd flown out of the cabin in a hurry. It wasn't a problem. There was a tub of three-bean chili in the fridge, along with—amazingly—some vegan sour cream.

Soon they were sitting cross-legged on a rug in front of the fire, enjoying the chili out of crispy taco bowls created by Harper.

Kat decided that the taco bowls were the best cooking invention ever. Yummy *and* they saved on the washing up. "Where did you learn to make these?"

"It's a Cuban recipe. I think my mom taught my dad and he taught me. Sometimes I wish she'd been around longer to teach me things herself, instead of being stolen by a stupid fever in a Costa Rican jungle, but then I remember how lucky I am to have the best father ever. A forgetful father, but no one's perfect."

Kat rarely gave her own absent dad a thought and sometimes felt guilty about it. Before she was even born, he'd made the fateful decision to surf a twenty-meter wave in Portugal. He'd never returned to shore. There was a photo of him on the mantelpiece in Bluebell Bay. On the rare occasions he did cross Kat's mind, that was how she pictured him: carefree and careless as he rode a breaker into the sunset.

Kat shut him out of her head. "I feel the same way about my mum. She's the best mother on earth, and I get her all to myself . . . except for a few thousand patients. And she gets me all to herself—except for you and Tiny, of course."

"Your mom's awesome," agreed Harper. "And any time you need a dad for anything, you're welcome to share mine."

Kat had a sudden recollection of her own spontaneous offer of friendship to a near stranger in the forest. A curious, wistful expression had flashed across Riley's face. *I wish* . . . , she'd begun. The wind had blown away that wish. Now Kat would always wonder what she'd meant to say.

"My mum already thinks of you as her second daughter," she told Harper. "I guess that sort of makes us family."

"Not sort of," her best friend said firmly. "We *are* family."

Harper's phone cheeped. "Message from Dad. He's flying to New York tomorrow and should be with us by

51

lunchtime on Tuesday. I can't wait till we're all together again."

"Neither can I," said Kat, worrying anew about her mum left alone at the wind-battered gas station.

While Harper hunted for dessert, Kat added another log to the fire. She was about to toss in some scraps of newspaper when a sidebar story leaped out at her: WISH LIST GANG PRIME SUSPECTS IN THEFT OF $50M DIAMOND NECKLACE.

The article was dated September 28, only a couple of weeks earlier. Kat read it aloud to Harper.

> "The starry opening of the Royal Manhattan Hotel's east wing ended in high drama last night when a $50 million diamond necklace belonging to Cynthia Hollinghurst, heiress to the Hollinghurst fortune, was snatched in the crowded ballroom.
>
> "The New York Police Department refused to confirm reports that clues found at the scene point to the notorious Wish List gang. The thieves are prime suspects in at least eight other high-profile heists ranging from Florida to Vermont. At each, they've left a wish list of multimillion-dollar goodies. Rare art, guitars, and a Ming vase have all fallen prey to their cunning.

"The diamond necklace was stolen at around 11:00 P.M. at the arctic-themed event. As waiters served smoking trays of ice cream made with liquid nitrogen to celebrities, politicians, and artists, there was a scream. Ms. Hollinghurst's precious gems were gone.

"A male suspect is helping police with their inquiries.

"Even before the theft, the event had been a PR disaster for the Royal Manhattan. It began with four climate-change activists being evicted after taking a blowtorch to a polar bear ice sculpture.

"Next, the advertised lobster canapés had to be substituted with pizza after a rogue kitchen hand and unidentified accomplice 'liberated' the lobsters from a tank.

"But the Royal Manhattan's woes were nothing compared to those of Force 10 Security, whose elite guards were responsible for the safekeeping of Ms. Hollinghurst's necklace.

"Asked how the diamond necklace came to be snatched from under the noses of five guards in a packed room, Force 10 CEO Tony Marmosett claimed that at the time, the men were being Good Samaritans.

"'I'm sorry about the diamonds—you have no idea how sorry. But how can I punish my guards for battling a blaze at a shop across the street till firefighters came on the scene? They rescued a military veteran suffering from smoke inhalation after his wheelchair got lodged in a steel grid. Frankly, I'm proud of them.'

"Clancy Hollinghurst, Cynthia's father, is offering a $1 million reward for the recovery of the necklace. He refused to comment on rumors that he's suing the hotel and Force 10 Security for untold millions."

Harper handed Kat a bowl of canned peaches and coconut ice cream. "What I want to know is how a ninety-one-year-old came to be hanging out with celebrities and politicians at a glitzy hotel event. Did nobody at Shady Oaks notice that Gerry Meeks was missing or raise the alarm? Don't those places have a duty of care to frail and muddled seniors?"

Kat savored a peach before replying. "I'd like to know why there are only nine items on the wish list."

"What do you mean?"

"It's an odd number. When the gang was dreaming up Ming vases or whatever to steal, you'd think they'd have come up with a round number: ten items, or twenty. Why nine?"

"Maybe they were planning a tenth heist, but before it could happen, Gerry Meeks was arrested."

"Not according to Brenda from the Sleepy-Time Inn. She told us that the wish list only ever had nine items on it."

Harper's phone rang. "Your mum," she mouthed at Kat, who put it on speaker. The connection was crackly and kept breaking up. The rain and wind roared in the background.

"Darling girl, sorry it's taken me forever to call . . . bit of a disaster . . . special part needed for the car . . . Only available in Lake Placid . . . Driving conditions hazardous, especially in the dark. Have been advised to spend the night in a hotel there . . ."

"*Spend the night?*" Kat couldn't believe it. Their vacation seemed cursed. "What time do you think you'll be able to get here tomorrow?"

"Depends when the mechanic can fit the part . . . Will keep you posted . . . Frustrating but nothing I can do . . . Kat, would you put Annette Brody on the line? I want to make sure she's able to take care of you both until . . ."

The line went dead. Kat tried calling back, but the signal was too feeble.

"Look on the bright side," said Harper. "If our parents had a clue that we were on our own in a remote cabin with a nor'easter raging, they'd be freaking out."

"Hmm. Good point."

To discourage her mum from ringing back, Kat wrote a carefully worded text.

No probs, Mum. We're warm & safe. Mrs. Brody made a delish 3-bean chili for our dinner & Harper conjured up ace taco bowls to go with it. Wish you'd been here. Have a nice night in Lake Placid. Be placid and DON'T WORRY!!! We're having a brilliant time xxx

The reply came in seconds.

Wonderful! Pass on my thanks to Mrs. Brody. Glad you're having fun. See you tomorrow. Sweet dreams. Love Mum xxx P.S. Tina says Tiny is missing you and sends lots of purrs and cuddles x

"Well, you got your wish," said Harper when Kat put down the phone. "We're alone in the wilderness. Now what?"

Harper's hazel eyes sparkled with mischief. "Pity we

don't have any mysteries to investigate. It's about time our Wolfe and Lamb detective agency had a new case to solve."

Kat picked up the crumpled story on the stolen diamond necklace. "Maybe we do."

MIDNIGHT VISITOR

KAT SAT UP IN BED, ADRENALINE PUMPING. "What was that?"

"Not again," groaned Harper. "Kat, this is an old log cabin. Loose tiles are going to bang, floorboards will creak even when no one's walking on them, and the wind's going to keep whining like an unhappy ghost. Put some earplugs in and close your eyes."

"It wasn't the wind," Kat said stubbornly. "It was a living creature, howling in the forest. Possibly more than one. The howls were different."

"I'll be the one howling if I don't get some sleep," complained Harper. She put a pillow over her head.

Moments later, a bone-chilling keening penetrated the memory foam. She flung aside the pillow. "What was that?"

"Told you so," said Kat, who hadn't moved. "There's something out there."

"Nobody told us there'd be wolves," said Harper in alarm.

Kat lifted the blinds and stared hard into the darkness, but the night held tight to its secrets. "What's weird is that the survival book I bought claimed there hadn't been a wolf pack in the Adirondacks since the 1890s. And no lone wolves have been seen in over a decade."

Yet she was as certain as Harper that they hadn't imagined the eerie sound. What was it? A bear in a snare? A loon in peril? Feral dogs out hunting?

The girls strained their ears. Whatever it was had gone quiet.

Kat's eyelids drooped and she burrowed beneath her moose-patterned duvet. "Wish there *were* wolves in the Adirondacks. I love them so much. They sing, you know, like we do, for the pure joy of it."

"Sing? Wolves?"

"They croon to their loved ones. It's a bonding ritual called social gluing. People see wolves as vicious killers, but they're the opposite. Their families are their whole world. They're so affectionate and protective of one another."

She murmured drowsily, "Per'aps there are wolves in our forest. They've sensed that there's a new Wolfe in the town and they're singing to welcome me . . ."

On that cheerful note, she fell asleep.

Harper smiled and lay down but found it impossible to drift off. The threat of wolves brought home the reality of lonely cabins in the wilderness. Every screech, thud, or rustle set her nerves jangling. She shot up in bed. "What was that?"

Kat didn't stir.

"Kat, something smashed in the kitchen. What if it's a burglar breaking in? Oh, please wake up. I'm worried."

But jet lag had caught up with Kat. She was unconscious.

Harper did her best to stay calm and rational. Before turning in, she and Kat had made certain that every door and window was secured. Even if they'd missed one, the fury of the gale would surely have been enough to put off any intruder without a hankering to be crushed by a falling tree or trampled by a frightened wild animal.

The noise came again—a distinct clinking.

Harper swung out of bed. She'd have to investigate. Alone.

"I'm a detective," Harper told herself. "If I'm to fight international criminals in real life as well as online, I can't let a petty thief faze me."

Arming herself with a wooden squirrel carving, she crept down the stairs. The clinking and clanking grew louder. Twice, Harper nearly ran screaming back to Kat. She forced herself on, muttering under her breath,

"Detective Lamb, you are fearless, fit, and fifty times cleverer than any burglar. You can do this."

Halfway down the stairs, she heard slurping. Someone or something was eating in their kitchen. That raised a fresh possibility for which Harper was utterly unprepared. What if she came face-to-face with a bear? Her father had told her a story about a bear breaking into a cabin in Canada, raiding the fridge, and then playing the piano—only not very well.

With no piano or rifle to distract it, this bear might claw her to pieces.

Would a wooden squirrel work as a bear-spray substitute? Harper suspected not. She had visions of flinging the carving behind her as a six-hundred-pound bear pounded after her.

An animated chittering suddenly echoed down the stairwell. Harper stifled a giggle. It was years since she'd heard that chittering, but she'd have recognized it anywhere.

Tiptoeing down the remaining steps, she caught the masked bandit red-pawed.

A raccoon was on the breakfast bar, licking peach nectar out of a can. Its nose and fur were sticky with juice and the remnants of the three-bean chili. Its eyelids fluttered with bliss.

The kitchen was a disaster zone. With no one to supervise, Harper and Kat had gone to bed without clearing up. The raccoon had taken full advantage of their laziness and of their leftovers. The chili pot was upended, dribbling sauce down the side of the stove. Ice-cream footprints traced an erratic journey around the living room. Taco crumbs and rice were strewn from one end of the kitchen to the other. A mug and a plate were in pieces.

The fridge was wide-open. On the tiles below, gnawed veggies swam in a pool of ketchup, maple syrup, and chips of china.

As Harper looked on in fascinated horror, the raccoon took an apple from the fruit bowl and washed it in a glass of water. When it caught sight of her, its expression was priceless. Abandoning the apple, it twisted off the countertop, adding a shattered glass to the ghastly stew on the tiles. It dived behind a cabinet and was gone.

Despite the mess, the relief of finding a raccoon in the cabin rather than a knife-wielding burglar left Harper elated. She'd faced her fears and won. She was practically a superhero.

Cleaning the kitchen took ages. After stoking the fire until it crackled and popped, Harper poured herself a glass of milk and opened a packet of Oreo cookies. Then she stretched out on the sofa with the TV remote.

The shutters were still banging, the wind still whining, and there were still unexplained creaks and groans, but Harper was no longer afraid. Not at all. Isolated cabins in the wilderness agreed with her, she decided. She couldn't wait for morning when she and Kat could explore the forest.

The news bellowed out at her. The polar vortex hurtling in from the Arctic had turned into a winter storm, now named Storm Mindy, after reaching wind speeds of close to ninety miles per hour on the northeast coast. There was footage of cars and houses buried under snow and a lighthouse beaming through a blizzard.

Harper lowered the volume and hopped up to get more cookies. Returning to the sofa, she was about to switch channels when an image of Gerry Meeks popped up, captioned: VILLAIN OR VICTIM?

A newscaster in an orange tie said, "On Monday, Gerry Thomas Meeks, a retired insurance salesman and the alleged leader of the Wish List gang, was charged with stealing a fifty-million-dollar diamond necklace from heiress Cynthia Hollinghurst.

"The ninety-one-year-old and his unknown accomplices are the prime suspects in nine high-profile heists across the United States. At the scene of each robbery, they left a wish list written with colored Sharpies. The wish list was simple, their alleged crimes not so much."

A graphic flashed up: Harper took a screengrab on her phone.

IS THIS THE REAL WISH LIST?

1. 1964 Fender Stratocaster Guitar Played by Bob Dylan
2. Green-Enameled Ming "Dragon" Vase
3. 1913 Liberty Head Nickel
4. Lost Eighteenth-Century Masterpiece by Sofia Rossi
5. Autographed First Edition of *Where the Wild Things Are* by Maurice Sendak
6. Fifth-Century Bronze Sculpture of a Horse and Hare
7. 1918 Inverted Jenny Stamp
8. Dress Worn by Audrey Hepburn in *My Fair Lady*
9. $50,000,000 Hollinghurst Diamond Necklace

An earnest reporter took up the story outside Shady Oaks Nursing Home. "Fresh doubts have been raised over the innocence of accused criminal mastermind Gerry Meeks after it emerged that at least three women, all calling themselves Mrs. A. Relative, signed him out of Shady Oaks Nursing Home for weekend breaks. Were they con artists or accomplices? Detectives are investigating."

Three grainy black-and-white CCTV images filled the screen. One woman was petite; one long-limbed and elegant; and one had thick, curly hair. All wore hats, and none of their faces were visible.

"Earlier, I spoke with the Shady Oaks director, Sylvia Jarman," said the reporter. "Ms. Jarman, does Mr. Meeks have any relatives?"

"No, he does not. He was devoted to his granddaughter, but she passed away many years ago."

"Yet your staff allowed a man with no family to disappear for weekends with three women bearing no resemblance to one another, each called Mrs. A. Relative?"

Sylvia Jarman eyed him severely over the top of her glasses. "Mike, our residents are grown-ups, not children, and we treat them as such. The visitors were courteous, and Gerry greatly looked forward to these outings. When he returned, he seemed . . . normal. Nothing aroused our suspicions. After his arrest, we found nothing incriminating in his room."

The reporter was like a dog with a chew toy. "You're telling me that you had no problem with one of your most fragile residents going partying till the wee hours at the Royal Manhattan?"

Standing before the Shady Oaks sign, Sylvia shuffled in her gel-soled shoes. "We were under the impression that he was having root-canal surgery under a general anesthetic, due to his advanced years, and would be in the hospital overnight."

"Being taken care of by *a relative,* no doubt," the reporter said nastily. "So every time Gerry left Shady Oaks with one of these accomplices or con artists, he might have been on his way to steal a priceless sculpture or Bob Dylan's guitar?"

"Absolutely not." Sylvia Jarman was indignant. "According to our records, he was absent on only one other date that coincides with the crimes of the so-called Wish List gang: a weekend when a stamp was stolen in Key West. I'm certain that police will find Gerry has a cast-iron alibi for that time too. On all other occasions, he was here at Shady Oaks, sitting in a quiet corner reading *Trouble Is My Business* or some such mystery."

She adjusted her glasses. "Mike, the Gerry Meeks we know is boringly ordinary. This is all a dreadful misunderstanding. When he's found innocent, as he will be, we'll welcome him home to Shady Oaks with open arms."

Harper switched off the TV. If only her dad had allowed her to bring her laptop. The Wish List case intrigued her. She itched to be able to investigate it. Even if she'd had her usual smartphone rather than the Stone Age Nokia her father had insisted she bring, hacking into the Shady Oaks server would have been as easy for her as counting to ten in French. If Gerry Meeks had emailed anyone ever, chances were Harper would have found it.

Then she remembered that there was no Wi-Fi at

the cabin. They'd come to the Adirondacks to get away from their phones and back to nature.

Harper grimaced. With no internet or data and only a pitiful signal on her non-smartphone, Detectives Wolfe and Lamb would not be solving cases any time soon.

It was her last thought before she fell asleep. When next she opened her eyes, it was nearly 8:00 A.M. Extricating herself from the deep folds of the sofa, she stood, stretched, and did a double take. Snowflakes were whirling past the window.

Overnight, Mirror Lake and the mountain had been transformed. Delicate snowflakes clung to the glass like butterflies. Others melted into the lake or formed frosting on outstretched branches.

A warm feeling filled Harper's chest. Living in the U.K., she'd forgotten how much she missed proper snow. Great, billowing piles of it. Snowball fights! Massive grinning snowmen!

Unexpectedly, she and Kat were going to be treated to a bonus winter holiday. What fun they'd have outside. They could make snow angels or pelt each other with snowballs to their heart's content.

The best part? There wasn't an adult in miles to tell them not to.

WOLVES

"I CAN'T BELIEVE YOU DIDN'T WAKE ME," said Kat—again—as they tucked into buttermilk pancakes made from a ready mix Harper had found in a cupboard. "New developments in our Wish List case, magical snow, and a live raccoon sitting right where my plate is. I slept through them all."

Harper reached for the maple syrup. "Believe me, I tried. There are five-thousand-year-old mummies in Egypt that have more life in them than you with jet lag. Anyhow, you should be thanking me, not picking on me. I risked my life to save you from a masked intruder."

"It was a harmless raccoon!"

"Yeah, but it might have been a masked assassin, and then where would you be? And I did save you from hours of cleaning. By the time Rocky the Rascal was done with the place, it needed the services of a biohazard team."

"Rocky?"

"That's what I've named our raccoon. You'll meet him, Kat. He'll be back. I got the feeling it wasn't his first time raiding the refrigerator."

"You think he squeezed behind that cabinet?"

Kat went to inspect it. "There's a missing floorboard between the wall and cabinet. Rocky must be using it as a bolt-hole. Wonder where it leads. Hope he has a warm den. It's getting colder by the minute."

Beyond the wall of glass, the white-and-mauve mountain and spiky trees were fuzzily mirrored in the lake. Snow swirled madly. Kat had the sensation of being in a vigorously shaken snow globe. It was dizzying.

She returned to her pancake. "Tell me about the story on the news. Did you learn anything more about the Wish List gang?"

"Only that Gerry Meeks was regularly signed out of Shady Oaks by three different women, all calling themselves Mrs. A. Relative."

"You're kidding?"

"Nope. Apparently, they don't even look alike. Also, only two of the dates that Gerry was gone for the weekend match up with any of the robberies. The other was when a postage stamp was stolen in Florida."

"A stamp?"

"Uh-huh. It's called the Inverted Jenny because the mail plane on it was accidentally printed upside down. I used to collect stamps, so I know it's worth a lot. Not as much as the diamond necklace, but a cool million, I'd say."

Kat was stunned. "A million dollars for one badly printed stamp? That's nuts."

"I don't make the rules."

"I just find it difficult to believe that Gerry Meeks is a hard-boiled diamond and stamp robber. Why would a ninety-one-year-old go on a crime spree? What's he going to spend fifty-one million dollars on? Two Ferraris? A yacht? And his own private jet and Caribbean island?"

"Who knows?" said Harper. "What I *can* tell you is senior-citizen crimes are on the rise. Me and Dad watched a program about it. Ever heard of the Hatton Garden safe-deposit robbery in London? There's a movie based on it. Six thieves in their sixties and seventies stole two hundred million pounds' worth of stuff. In the U.S., we had a ninety-two-year-old bank robber called Hunter Rountree. He'd hand tellers a note with 'Robbery' written on it and walk out with thousands."

Kat was unsure. "Thousands is one thing. Snatching a fifty-million-dollar necklace from an heiress in a ballroom packed with celebrities and armed guards is a whole other league. Gerry doesn't seem the type."

"Agreed," said Harper. "If he did it, he must have

had help. Shame I don't have my laptop. We could have taken a peek at the Royal Manhattan's website. They might have posted images from the event on September twenty-seventh. Pictures are worth a thousand words. Between us, we might have spotted a few clues.

"Without online digging, all we know about Gerry is that he's a retired insurance salesman who's 'boringly ordinary.' That's how the Shady Oaks director described him. Says he mostly sits in a quiet corner reading books like *Trouble Is My Business*."

"What's that?" asked Kat.

"A detective novel by Raymond Chandler, one of America's most famous novelists. He wrote mysteries about Philip Marlowe, a private investigator in L.A."

"That's the opposite of boring," said Kat with a grin. "Nothing dull about solving mysteries!"

"Well, *we* can't solve the Wish List mystery." Harper was suddenly sulky. "Not here, stuck in a snowbound cabin with no Wi-Fi."

Kat was amused. "The trouble with you computer geniuses is you're too reliant on technology."

Harper scowled. "You haven't complained before."

"And I'm not complaining now," Kat said patiently. "You're one of the best hackers anywhere. We'd never have solved a single mystery without your help. But this is the perfect opportunity to practice some good old-fashioned detective work."

"How? It's not as if we can get to a library or ask questions in the local village. With no phone data or internet, we can't even contact Edith to ask her to do our research for us."

Edith Chalmers was a retired librarian in Bluebell Bay. They'd helped her while investigating their first case. These days, using the impressive resources of her Armchair Adventurers' Club library, she was more likely to help them. She and Kai Liu, another client who'd since become a friend, were Kat and Harper's deputies in their fight against crime.

But even the bravest, most dedicated deputy was no use if there was no way of contacting them.

"Before smartphones and the internet, detectives often began their investigations by going through the archives," said Kat. "I'll check the newspapers in the wood basket. There might be an article or two on the other Wish List robberies. We could also take a look at the bookcase on the landing. Between the thrillers and travel guides, there might be something useful on bronze statues or Bob Dylan's guitars."

Harper's blues were banished. "You're so right! Philip Marlowe, Poirot, Nancy Drew, Miss Marple, and Sherlock Holmes—i.e., the greatest detectives *ever*—didn't need laptops and five-G connections to crack crimes. Nor do we. Where should I begin? What old-fashioned method should we try first?"

Kat laughed. "Who said anything about work? It's the first day of our holiday, and winter's somehow arrived in the middle of fall. Let's get creative and make a toboggan."

"Are you sure this is a good idea?" worried Kat as they struggled to carry an inflatable mattress up the hill behind the cabin. They were wearing borrowed, oversized snow boots, but it was hard work pushing through knee-deep snow.

From the bedroom window, Harper had spotted a fire break—a cleared strip-cutting through the dense forest. It would, she'd decided, make an excellent ski slope.

Kat wasn't so sure. "What if we can't stop and smack into a pine or skid into the lake?"

"We're not attempting the Olympic ski jump," Harper said playfully. "Basically, this is a nursery slope. There's zero chance of us soaring into Mirror Lake or breaking a limb on a tree. Okay, maybe not zero, but the risk is teensy-weensy."

Kat was in no way reassured. "Let's nip back to the cabin and check the weather report before we go farther. What if there's a snow squall?"

Harper lowered her side of the mattress. "I'm guessing you've never been skiing."

"What's that got to do with anything?"

"Ever tried tobogganing?"

"Never."

"You're in for a treat. Don't stress about the weather. We'll check the app when we get back. Just trust me."

On balance, trusting Harper had always worked out for the best. Kat decided there was no harm in doing it again. "All right, I will."

Their first run down the slope was an unqualified success. The mattress was supremely comfortable. It gave them a silky smooth, exhilaratingly fast ride before dumping them in a soft pile of snow at the bottom of the hill.

Kat was glowing. "Harper, you're a toboggan genius as well as a computer genius. That was the best experience ever. Let's go again, from higher up."

"Not too high," laughed Harper, pink-cheeked and euphoric. "It's not like we have brakes. If we lose control, we really could end up in the lake."

They puffed up the hill, their breath making misty speech bubbles. Kat was grateful for Riley's merino wool neckerchief. The air was as fresh and biting as toothpaste: minty with pine.

The farther they climbed, the trickier it was to find a run clear of small obstacles and with enough snow to give them a smooth ride. By the time they found a suitable launchpad, the distant cabin looked unnervingly small.

Kat sat on the back of their toboggan. She wrapped

one arm tightly around Harper's waist and gripped the thin branches of a frosty shrub with her left mitten. It was the only thing anchoring them to the slope.

"I'll count to three," said Harper, who regretted agreeing to the advanced slope but wasn't about to admit it. "Don't let go of the shrub until I say so."

"Aye, aye, Captain Lamb," sang Kat to hide her nerves.

"One . . . two—"

"Wait!"

"What?!" cried Harper.

"I saw something slink through the trees. On the right, halfway down the slope."

"A moose? A bobcat? What?"

"It's probably nothing," said Kat. "Let's go."

"Sure?"

"Sure."

"One . . . two—"

A heartrending howl rose from the valley floor, chilling them to the marrow. A chorus of ghostly howls followed.

"Wolves!" panicked Harper. "A whole pack of them. Kat, what are we going to do? They'll eat us alive."

At that precise second, the shrub they were using as a handbrake tore loose from the ground. The mattress shot forward like a gravity-powered bobsled. Taken unawares, the girls tipped backward. They had to fight to stay aboard.

With little wind resistance, the homemade toboggan was greased lightning in action. It skimmed the surface of the snow, ramping every mound and ripple. The girls clung on for dear life, too petrified to scream.

Just when it seemed that it might actually take flight, their runaway craft clipped an unseen rock, skewed sideways, and headed straight for a tree.

"Bail, bail, bail!" yelled Harper. The mattress flipped and did it for them. It was like being boosted from the ejector seat of an F-14 jet.

Kat thudded down and rolled and rolled until she collided with a prickly but snow-softened bush. She lay winded for so long that icy flakes collected in her eyelashes. Gingerly, she moved her fingers and toes. Apart from a persistent growling in her ears, she appeared to be unhurt. She got up shakily.

"Kat, look out! Behind you!"

Harper was crawling out of a snow-filled hollow, her face as white as the landscape.

Beneath her woolly hat, Kat's scalp prickled with fear. She spun around. The growling wasn't in her head. It issued from a clump of bushes. Through the snow-flecked greenery, Kat made out glaring blue eyes and a ripple of gray fur. The creature fled, limping.

Wincing, Kat started after it. Crimson specks marked its escape through the trees.

Harper ran to catch up with her, grabbing Kat's

arm. "Are you out of your mind? That must be the beast we heard last night. Forget that nonsense about wolves enjoying singing. You'll be savaged."

Kat tugged away. "It's not a wolf, it's an injured husky. I have to help it."

"Then let's call the emergency services or a local veterinarian. We've already had one near-death experience today. I don't want another."

A cacophony of howling drowned out her words. Bloody pawprints led to a well-worn track, ending at a high chain-link fence, a short distance from Nightingale Lodge. Behind it were five huskies. Two were growling, two wagged their tails, and one raced around in ecstatic circles.

A sixth husky was on the wrong side of the fence. Her right forepaw was tucked up beneath her. As she bared her fangs, she trembled with pain and cold.

"Alaskan and Siberian huskies," said Kat. "One hurt and all hungry. Somebody forgot to tell us that they're ours for the holidays."

WRONG TURN

"I DON'T UNDERSTAND," SAID HARPER, poking at the fire until it spat sparks. "Did we miss something? Was some instruction lost in translation? How were we not aware that we were supposed to feed six huskies?"

Kat was on the sofa with the wounded husky, expertly bandaging its paw with the help of the small first aid kit she'd brought in her luggage. "It doesn't matter who messed up, does it?" she cooed to the dog, leaning down to kiss it on the nose. "What matters is that we get to hang out with you and your gorgeous friends."

Harper stared at her incredulously. "How do you do that? How do you win them over so fast?"

Kat shrugged. "My mum's a vet. I've had animal emergency training from the best. I could treat a cut paw when I was six."

"I don't just mean the physical stuff," said Harper. "It's as if you read their minds. Half an hour ago, that husky was ready to tear you to pieces. Now she's a pussycat."

Kat secured the bandage with micropore tape and hugged the husky close. "You have to let them know you're on their side. That's the most important thing. Animals' hearts are pure, but their trust is easy to lose. If I'd lied to her, told her, 'Don't worry, this won't hurt a bit,' and then she was in agony, next time she wouldn't believe me."

Harper sat on the arm of the sofa. "So, what *did* you tell her?"

"I said, 'I'm going to disinfect and tape up your paw. It'll hurt like hell, but we'll get through it together, and I promise you'll feel heaps better afterward. And when it's over, I'll give you a scrumptious dinner and tons of cuddles.'"

"You told her all of that?"

Kat smiled. "Didn't have to. I thought it, and she picked up on it. Animals are the real mind readers. Most times, they know us better than we know ourselves. I only hope that the part about dinner is true. We need to find their food."

"On it." Harper returned to the kitchen to search. This time she realized that a tall framed poster of racing huskies hid a door with no handle. She pulled at the frame to open it. Taped to the other side of the door was a sheet printed with each husky's name and the quantity of biscuits and meat (60 percent chicken, 40 percent beef) he or she ate daily.

"Jackpot! Husky chow and feeding instructions."

Kat was relieved. A starving-husky crisis was one they could do without. She left her new friend on the sofa and laid out six bowls. Watching the husky for reaction, she read the names out loud: "Matty, Fleet, Rebel, Thunder, Nomad, and Dancer."

On hearing her name, Nomad sat to attention.

"Good name for a wanderer," approved Kat. "Huskies have a reputation for being escape artists. Nomad's obviously the Houdini of the pack. She must have cut her paw getting out of the kennels to try to find her owner. Harper, are you sure your dad didn't drop any hints about huskies at Nightingale Lodge? Could he have been saving them as a surprise for us?"

Harper wrinkled her nose. "Dad's hopeless at keeping secrets, but I suppose it's possible that he and your mom were in on it together. With the stress of the car breaking down and having to go to Lake Placid, maybe your mom forgot to ask us to feed them."

"Possibly," said Kat, knowing full well that an earthquake wouldn't erase six hungry dogs from her mother's mind. "Or if these are racing huskies, maybe Ross Ryan didn't trust anyone except Mrs. Brody to take care of them. But then why didn't she mention them when she messaged earlier to say she wouldn't be able to get back here today because the snowy roads were too treacherous?"

Even as she spoke, Kat knew that the mystery of the huskies had nothing to do with Mrs. Brody's travel difficulties. Something was wrong with Nightingale Lodge. She just couldn't work out what.

Judging by the way Harper was drumming the arm of the chair and nervously jiggling a foot, her best friend was performing similar contortions trying to make the story they'd told themselves fit.

"I'll send Dad a text, thanking him for the surprise but not saying what surprise I mean," Harper said cheerfully. "See what he says."

"And I'll dish up the dogs' dinners." Kat cast a troubled glance out the window. "If the weather gets any worse, we'll have to bring them inside. Huskies have two coats and a metabolism designed to cope with harsh conditions, but even they have limits."

"That's fine with me. No threat of intruders if we have six domestic wolves and a raccoon keeping watch."

Two freezing relays to take food to the kennels, three hundred meters up the track, was enough to convince them that having the huskies in the cabin was the correct decision. According to the barometer hung from the porch railing, the temperature had dropped to 15 degrees.

Before the hour was up, the living room was freshly carpeted—in husky fur. Fleet, Matty, Dancer, and Thunder had made themselves at home on the sofas. Nomad and Rebel stretched out in front of the fire.

The girls were squashed up together in the armchair. As Harper flipped through TV channels in search of a weather forecast, her father's reply pinged in from London.

Hey kiddo, great to hear from you. As I write, I'm chewing on rubbery poached eggs in my glam (NOT) airport hotel. Storm Mindy is causing mayhem here too. All New York–bound flights are canceled or delayed. WILL get to you before it's time to come home even if I have to swim! Or ski!

Meantime your text made my day. I'm glad you're managing to have a good time despite my epic passport fail and Ross's car dying on you all.

I'm glad you like your surprise! I'm guessing you mean the waterfall behind Nightingale Lodge? I told Dr. Wolfe not to say anything because I thought you girls would get a kick out of it when

you discovered it. Can't wait to see it myself,
though if the forecast's accurate, it'll shortly be
wall-to-wall stalactites! Wrap up and take care.
Will call when I land at Newark. Love Dad x

The girls rose and moved like sleepwalkers to the window at the back of the cabin. They stared out at the snowy
hill. Through the pines, they could see the wooden corner
of the kennels and the track that led to them. There was
no telltale mist or rainbow. No muted roar.

"What waterfall?" said Harper.

"I knew it," ranted Harper. "Soon as we walked into
the cabin, I had a gut sense that something was off."

"So did I," said Kat. "I felt it in my bones."

"Then why didn't you say anything?"

"Why didn't you?" accused Kat.

Harper collapsed into the armchair. "We need to take
ten deep breaths. Whatever's gone wrong is not our fault."

Kat continued pacing. "The animals were the giveaway. If I hadn't been so exhausted when we arrived, I'd
have cottoned on sooner."

"What animals?"

"The bear lamps and moose cushions. The husky
cookie jar and squirrel dish towels."

"I know, I know," despaired Harper. "A whole safari
park and not a single nightingale. But who's the idiot
who watched TV last night, totally forgetting that the

main reason Dad rented Ross Ryan's cabin was because it has NO TELEVISION?"

"We're both idiots," Kat corrected her. "Didn't your dad describe Nightingale Lodge as a natural log cabin where we'd be able to lie in bed and gaze out over the lake?"

"Uh-huh. This cabin is red wood with a white trim and our room faces the hill at the back. But the biggest clues of all are our fluffy friends." She leaned over to rub the ears of Fleet, the smallest dog. "The real Nightingale Lodge has *no huskies*."

"We're the world's dumbest detectives," Harper raged. "If we can't detect that we're in the wrong cabin, what hope do we have of solving the Wish List mystery with no internet?"

It was only then that the full implications of their situation began to sink in.

"Never mind the Wish List gang," fretted Kat. "If the owner of this cabin catches us here, *we'll* be the ones on the news: being charged with breaking and entering. We're like Goldilocks in the 'Three Bears' story. We've moved into someone else's cabin, eaten their dinner, slept in their bed. Unlike the fairy tale, we've also stolen their dogs. How did we manage this?"

"It was the nightingale sign," Harper reminded her. "It was twisting in the wind and must have been facing the wrong direction. Jet took the right fork when he should have gone left. Those lights we saw on the other side of the lake, I'll bet one of them is Nightingale Lodge."

"Then we can fix this," cried Kat. "It's finally stopped snowing. Let's clean the cabin, put the huskies in their kennels, and hike around the lake with as much of our baggage as we can carry. The rest we can hide in the shed we saw out the back. If we hurry, we'll reach Nightingale Lodge before nightfall and before Mum arrives. We can pretend this was all a bad dream."

Hypnotized by events unfolding on the silent TV, Harper was no longer listening. She snatched up the remote. "Kat, the storm! It's coming for us."

A stern American boomed, "Weather forecasters are blaming a brand-new multibillion-dollar IT system upgrade for a glitch that had them predicting that Storm Mindy would track south after dumping record snow on New England, leaving thirty thousand without power.

"Instead, residents of Vermont and the Adirondack region, who were caught off guard by last night's nor'easter, are braced for an early blast of winter. Storm Mindy, the arctic beast that some are calling the Wolf from the North, has changed course and is bearing down on the northern Adirondacks. Officials are now scrambling to set up emergency shelters after the National Weather Service has issued a blizzard warning.

"Emergency services are gearing up for what could be

the worst October storm for decades. Isolated communities in the High Peaks, Blue Mountain Lake, and Raquette Lake areas could be cut off by whiteout conditions and nearly twelve inches of snow. Panic buying of fuel, bottled water, and core groceries emptied shelves in stores—"

Harper muted the voice of doom. "We can forget hiking to Nightingale Lodge. Those isolated communities? We're in one of them. If Mindy hits us tomorrow, it'll be a miracle if we don't have to dig our way out."

Her phone vibrated in her pocket. She handed it to Kat. "Message from your mom."

They read it together, Harper resting her chin on her friend's shoulder.

Dear Kat, you'll have heard by now that we've chosen the worst possible weather week to take a vacation in the Adirondacks. Storm Mindy is on her way and we're in her path! As if that wasn't bad enough, the car part I need is out of stock and has to be ordered. If it's not here by tomorrow, I'll rent a car. I did try my best to find a cabdriver willing to take me to Nightingale Lodge before the storm arrives, but it's impossible. Lake Placid's jammed with people seeking refuge from the big freeze or buying survival essentials. If Mrs. Brody wasn't with you, I'd be out of my mind with worry.

Thanks for being so understanding, darling.
Hope you don't get too bored stuck indoors
without TV or laptops. Spoke to Harper's father.
No doubt she's heard that her dad's flight has
been delayed till Wednesday night. We love you
both and are doing our best to get to you from
opposite ends of the globe. Mum xx

"Please don't tell her we're alone in a stranger's cabin,"
begged Harper. "Dad will have a nervous breakdown."

"As if," retorted Kat.

Hi Mum, sorry you're having a mare with
the car. We're snug here. The snow is soooo
beautiful. We have books, a blazing fire, and a
ton of food to help us survive Storm Mindy. I
only hope the forest creatures don't perish or
get blown to Alaska.

The huskies weren't in any danger of doing either.
Prone in front of the fire, Nomad was dreaming, her
fluffy ears twitching. Rebel yawned and started grooming
his immaculate white paws.

Kat ended:

Don't worry about us and we won't worry about
you! Stay warm and placid in Lake Placid till

> Mindy's gone. When we're all together, we'll
> have the best vacation ever. K & H xx

The text whooshed away. Kat and Harper sat in shocked disbelief. They were trapped in who knew whose cabin with who knew whose dogs, with the Wolf from the North poised to pounce. Whatever happened now, they had no hope of rescue.

Their winter wonderland had just become a nightmare.

STAR WITNESS

THE NEXT MORNING BROUGHT A DIAMOND-hard frost and a clear sky the infinite turquoise of an Antarctic ice sheet. The needle on the porch barometer had sunk to 5 degrees.

Harper was disconsolate. She kept running to the window to check for the flat, dark nimbostratus clouds that portend snow.

"Where's a good blizzard when you need one? Why is it sunny today of all days? Where is Storm Mindy? The sooner she dumps snow on the track to our cabin, the better I'll like it. No chance of the owner dropping in unexpectedly then."

She took off her glasses and rubbed her tired eyes. The snow glare hurt. She and Kat had barely slept. Huskies, it turned out, were doggy dynamos. If they weren't kept entertained 24/7, they invented their own games. Two cushions, a dog-training manual, and one of Harper's sneakers had already fallen victim to their eager jaws.

All night long, the huskies had taken it in turns to howl, whine, and scratch at the door for bathroom breaks or to chase one another over the furniture.

"Isn't there a dog-whispering technique you can use to control them?" pleaded Harper, leaping to save a lamp knocked over by boisterous Matty.

"Of course, but it won't solve the problem." Kat lay on the fireside rug between Nomad and Fleet. "Huskies hate being cooped up, especially if they're used to tons of exercise. See how lean and muscly these two are? Whoever owns them is either a fitness fanatic who takes them on marathon bike rides or runs, or a musher who—"

"What's a musher?"

"Someone who drives a dogsled. These huskies are so strong that it wouldn't surprise me if they're used to taking tourists on sled rides when the lake's frozen over."

Harper perked up. "If they belong to a musher, that person might be so appreciative that we've kept their dogs fed and alive, they won't mind a bit about the chewed cushions or book; or the broken mugs, plate, and glasses; or that we've been living in their home and eating their food."

"Possibly," said Kat without conviction. She kept

thinking about the Airstream trailer they'd passed on Otter Creek Road. The one with the sign framed by two painted guns: IF YOU'RE FOUND HERE TONIGHT, YOU'LL BE FOUND HERE IN THE MORNING.

What if their cabin was owned by someone who shot trespassers first and asked questions later?

Somehow, Kat doubted it. In a bid to find answers about who owned the cabin, she and Harper had searched every cupboard and drawer. There was nothing personal in the cabin. No family photos. No electricity bills or bits of string or dried-up pens. No kitschy knickknacks brought home from exotic travels. It looked and felt like a rental.

But who owned the dogs? Was it a seasonal worker such as a ski guide? There'd been fresh food in the fridge, so they'd obviously been expected. Had that person fallen ill or had car trouble too?

"I can't bear the suspense a second longer," said Harper, reaching for the remote yet again. "I have to know how Storm Mindy's progressing."

The primary colors of the TV popped out at them. The local news was just beginning. A banner scrolled across the bottom of the screen. Harper read it twice before she could take it in.

BREAKING NEWS: STAR WITNESS MISSING AND BODYGUARDS IN ICU AFTER WRONG TURN IN THE ADIRONDACKS

"Kat, our case! You've got to see this." She stabbed at the volume button.

A ghost of a frown fluttered across the newsreader's crease-free forehead as the story unfurled on her teleprompter.

"The star witness in the trial of alleged Wish List gang leader Gerry Meeks is missing, feared lost or the victim of foul play. It is believed that protection officers assigned to guard the witness took a wrong turn in the snow-hit Adirondack Park in upper New York State.

"The drama began early this morning when a snow-plow driver called nine-one-one to report an abandoned vehicle with the engine running. Paramedics attending the scene found a critically injured man and woman and evidence that a third person had been in the vehicle.

"The identity of the star witness in the high-profile Wish List gang trial has until now been a closely guarded secret. With Storm Mindy set to bring whiteout conditions to the northern Adirondacks later today, New York State detectives from the Bureau of Criminal Investigation have taken the unusual step of naming the witness due to her age and extreme vulnerability."

"No!" gasped Kat as a photo of a grinning girl in a pink baseball cap popped up. "No, that's impossible. Harper, that's Riley, the girl I told you about. The one who could mimic a loon and gave me her blue neckerchief."

"You're positive?"

"One hundred and ten percent. Remember me telling you that there was something distant and peculiar about her aunt and uncle? Now I understand why. They were police bodyguards, not relatives. I guess the 'cousins' they talked about weren't real either. Uh, what are you doing?"

Harper was on a chair squinting at the screen at close range. When she climbed down, footage of a black SUV in a forest clearing was being replaced by a picture of a handsome man in an expensive suit. Riley was beside him, scowling in an equally expensive dress.

The newsreader continued, "Riley Gabriella Matthews, twelve-year-old daughter of Daylesford Bank chairman Wainwright Matthews, was the sole witness to the theft of Cynthia Hollinghurst's fifty-million-dollar diamond necklace at the Royal Manhattan last month.

"Police have launched an appeal for witnesses to this morning's accident. Local volunteers with knowledge of the northern Adirondacks are urged to call this number if they can assist search-and-rescue teams . . ."

Harper killed the TV. "Where's the map?"

Kat was in tears. She couldn't bear the thought of the warm, funny girl who'd danced with her in the ruby rain being lost in the snowy wilderness.

The report didn't specify what "foul play" Riley might have fallen victim to, but Kat imagined it had something to do with the Wish List gang. Without a star witness to testify that Gerry Meeks had stolen the diamond necklace, the trial would collapse. Gerry would walk free from the court.

Had his accomplices ambushed the SUV and whisked Riley off to their lair? Or had she escaped into the forest, disoriented or injured?

Tears streamed down Kat's cheeks at the thought of Riley frozen, afraid, and at the mercy of kidnappers and wild animals. The American girl had talked of the trees and loons as if they were her only real friends. If she was lonely then, how must she feel now?

Kat had offered Riley Tiny's photo as a talisman of friendship and protection. Would his Savannah energy be enough to keep her safe from polar temperatures, charging bears, or ruthless kidnappers? It was a lot to ask of a cat on the other side of the Atlantic, even one as unique as Tiny.

Harper had nipped upstairs. She returned with a packet of Kleenex for Kat and the giant map. "I've seen it; I've definitely seen it."

"Sorry, you've lost me," mumbled Kat, blowing her nose.

"Pine Cove Road." Harper spread the map with shaking fingers. "I spotted the sign in the side-view mirror of the TV van filming the SUV. I'm sure I saw it when we were trying to find Otter Creek Road on Sunday, the day we arrived in the Adirondacks."

"Is it only Tuesday?" Kat said miserably. "Feels as if we've been here forever."

Harper bent over the map with a pencil. "This is the forest where you met Riley. This is the route we took afterward. I can see where we went wrong. We were driving in circles. Here's Otter Creek Road and Deadwood Bridge, and here's where we took the right fork instead of the left."

Kat sniffed. "That means Nightingale Lodge is on the other side of the lake like you thought. There's the waterfall your dad told us about. What does this have to do with Riley?"

"Got it!" Harper said in triumph, stabbing an olive-green patch with her pencil. "Pine Cove Road. This is where your friend disappeared. We can help look for her."

Kat's heart contracted at the word *friend*. As strange as it seemed, she did consider Riley a friend. Now her friend had disappeared.

"But we don't have a car. And Storm Mindy's on the way."

Harper was measuring the distance with a pencil. "It's a little over two miles if we follow this stream. It takes a fit person fifteen minutes to walk a mile. Say a little over thirty to walk two miles in this snow."

She glanced meaningfully at the huskies. Rebel was munching up his third cushion, Matty and Thunder were playing tag around the dining table, and Fleet was clawing at the door to go out. Only Nomad was behaving. She sat at Kat's feet, watching her anxiously.

Kat rushed to salvage the remains of the moose cushion from Rebel. "Are you thinking what I'm thinking? That we could take the huskies for a long walk so they can let off steam while we help look for Riley?"

"That's exactly what I'm thinking."

"What if we get caught in a snowstorm?"

"Mindy's not due till two P.M.," Harper said airily, as if she was discussing the visit of a favorite aunt. "If we leave now, we can search for a couple of hours and be back before she arrives. We'll stoke up the fire, batten down the hatches, and eat waffles till it blows over, or the cops arrive to arrest us for trespassing. Whichever comes first."

Kat longed to rescue Riley more than anything, but venturing into the wilderness with a snowstorm looming was not a stroll in a London park. She had the huskies to think about too. Until their owner turned up, it was her responsibility to keep them safe.

"What if Pine Cove Road is crawling with volunteers and police with dogs? The huskies might get into a fight and be bitten. And won't people be suspicious if they see two girls out alone with Storm Mindy coming?"

"No, because first glimpse we catch of anyone—human or animal—we run," Harper assured her. "The last thing we want is to be ringing your mom or my dad from a police cell or social services. But imagine if we detected some clue the professionals missed that led to Riley being saved? A locket in the snow. A torn button. *Something*."

Kat felt a surge of optimism. "Let's do it. I'll fetch the huskies' harnesses and put on my boots. If I was missing in the wilderness, I'd hope my friends would do everything in their power to find me. By the way, Harper, Riley's your friend too. I sort of volunteered you."

"That's sealed it, then. I have to help her." Harper wriggled into a fleece and tugged her jacket on over it. "If only we had Google Maps. Our biggest challenge is that we're not locals. We don't know the Adirondacks and we definitely don't know the woods."

"No," said Kat, "but the huskies do."

DOUBLE JEOPARDY

"I WANT IT ON RECORD THAT MY ARMS ARE two inches longer than they were when I left the house," complained Harper as she was towed along a slushy track by an overexcited Matty and Thunder. "When we're back in Bluebell Bay, we can visit Monkey World and I'll be able to make the orangutans jealous."

"Huskies are at their happiest when they're pulling," explained Kat, whose own biceps were being sorely tested by Rebel and Dancer. "That's why they love sled racing in Alaska. They're genetically programmed to run for hundreds of kilometers without tiring. They're not like some Labrador, content to while away his life gobbling treats and snoozing on a deluxe dog bed. Huskies have more in common with wolves."

"I'd never have guessed," panted Harper, as Matty

and Thunder lunged after an unsuspecting squirrel. It skittered away through the crispy white undergrowth.

Watching Harper struggle to hold the dogs back, Kat was thankful they'd left Nomad and Fleet guarding the cabin. Six huskies would have been two too many. She and Harper would have been hauled halfway to Canada by now.

On the plus side, the huskies kept them moving at a brisk pace. They'd been speed-walking for twenty-five minutes, following a stream sluggish with gray ice. Husky wrestling aside, it had been disturbingly simple. So far, the weather had been kind. Nothing and no one had impeded their progress.

It made Kat nervous. "Better keep the bear spray handy, Harper. I doubt we'll need it, but if we do, you'll have to be quicker on the draw than a Wild West gunfighter."

Harper stopped in her tracks. The huskies kept going and nearly pulled her over. "I thought *you* were bringing the bear spray."

"I thought *you* were bringing it."

Kat hid a twinge of alarm. "Never mind. With Storm Mindy on the way, every sensible bear in the Adirondacks will be scuttling for its hibernation burrow. If it wasn't for Riley, I'd be hibernating myself."

Harper glanced nervously over her shoulder. "No

bear would dare bother us with the huskies around, would it, Kat? Will the rattlesnakes be sleeping as well? Or will the snow make them even more lethal because they'll be sluggish with cold and won't wake up till we tread on them? Urgh, I hate snakes."

Kat, who did like snakes, giggled. "I read a funny story about an eighteenth-century rattlesnake hunter in the Adirondacks: Father Elisha. He captured hundreds of snakes with a forked stick and sold them all over as curiosities. Never got bitten until the day he went hunting in a smart jacket and white stockings."

"White stockings?"

"Uh-huh. He claimed he was only nipped because the 'varmints'—that's what he called them—mistook him for a local judge."

"How is that funny?" said Harper, annoyed. "Did Father Elisha die?"

"He did not."

"That's something, I suppose."

Kat grinned. "He died the next time he was bitten, despite wearing his usual scruffy clothes. The varmints didn't recognize him then either."

"That is the worst story I've ever heard," declared Harper. "Why would you tell me that when I'm walking through a rattlesnake-infested forest? Kat Wolfe, I'm not speaking to you for the rest of the day."

"Of course it's not funny that he *died*," said Kat,

laughing more at Harper's expression than the story. "It's funny that he thought he was bitten because they didn't recognize—"

"Shh!" Harper pressed a finger to her lips. The huskies' sensitive ears were trained forward, their black noses sniffing the air.

A distant engine started up. There was a ripple of navy blue between the trees as a truck accelerated. From this distance, it was impossible to tell whether it was driven by an official or a thrill seeker. The local police chief had warned drivers in the path of Storm Mindy not to use the roads unless it was a life-and-death emergency. That being the case, they assumed that the truck belonged to a police officer or member of the search team.

The dogs began to bark hysterically and leap around. Kat dropped to her knees in the snow. They swarmed around her. She hugged each in turn and whispered in their ears.

Harper forgot to be angry and watched in amazement. When Kat finally stood up, the huskies were no longer unruly. They were silent and focused: on high alert.

Girls and dogs proceeded with caution, in a tight group. As they approached Pine Cove Road and the crime scene, Kat and Harper kept a wary watch for guards. The huskies never broke pace. They were sure there were none.

If the tire tracks, boot prints, and dirty snow were anything to go by, there'd been a great deal of coming and going in the hours since the bodyguards' SUV was discovered.

"It could have been pitch-dark when Riley's protection team made a wrong turn," said Harper. "Why in the world would they have gotten out of the vehicle here, in a wilderness packed with dangers?"

"Two theories," said Kat.

"Go on."

"Their GPS failed, and they were attacked by a random maniac after stopping to ask for directions. There are no houses around, so whoever they encountered was likely on a motorbike or in a vehicle. During the struggle, Riley escaped into the forest. She knew this area so well that she thought of the trees and birds as friends. If she was afraid for her life, she'd have believed that her best chance of survival was in the forest."

"Not if she wasn't wearing thermals," Harper pointed out. "Maybe the reason the protection officers were on the road so early is because they discovered their safe house wasn't safe anymore. If they bundled Riley into the vehicle in her pajamas and if she wasn't able to grab anything warm before running to hide, she'd have been at grave risk of hypothermia. What's your second theory?"

"That the bodyguards were flagged down by someone they knew and trusted, or by a person pretending to be in trouble," said Kat. "A Wish List gang member might have followed them, cut in front of them, and then pretended that his car had broken down. Maybe Riley's bodyguards got out of their vehicle to try to assist them."

"Good Samaritans," mused Harper. "Interesting. That's what happened on the night of the diamond robbery too. The Force Ten guards were across the street fighting a fire. They were being Good Samaritans."

She checked her watch. "We'd better move if we're going to find Riley. Storm Mindy will be here in three hours. By then, we need to be in our cabin with the doors bolted and the shutters nailed down."

She threw a disgusted glance at the muddy mess of boot treads, skid marks, and a couple of candy wrappers. "Should we give up now? Looks as if every cop and volunteer in the Adirondacks has trampled through these woods. Fat chance of finding any clues. Sherlock Holmes and Philip Marlowe had it so much easier in their day."

Kat was tempted. The huskies were bored and bursting with energy. They'd already forgotten their manners. But she knew she'd never forgive herself if she hadn't done everything possible to rescue her friend. "Hold on. I have an idea."

She took off the blue neckerchief. "Let's see if any

of the huskies pick up Riley's scent. Police sniffer dogs need years of training, so I doubt it'll work."

"Won't the cops already have tried that?" asked Harper.

"Probably, but not necessarily. The storm's messed everything up. The dog unit could be busy hauling people out of the snow in Vermont and the other end of the Adirondacks."

Matty was the only husky to show any interest in the neckerchief, but when Kat instructed her to track the missing girl, she rushed straight over to the discarded wrappers. She dragged Kat around and around the clearing.

Harper, who was standing still, was in danger of frostbite and losing the will to live when Kat showed Matty the neckerchief one last time. At long last, something clicked. Matty turned and loped into the forest, dragging Kat, who was still clinging to Rebel, through a thornbush.

"How do we know that she's following Riley's scent and not just leading us on a wild-husky chase?" demanded Harper.

"We don't" was Kat's honest response. "But if there's a one-in-a-million chance that she is on Riley's trail, I'm willing to risk it. Can you manage the other three huskies if we go on ahead?"

She thrust Rebel's leash at Harper and was gone without waiting for a reply.

At first, Harper wasn't too concerned. Thunder, Dancer, and Rebel trotted faithfully after their friend. They could hear Matty and Kat long after Harper could not.

But with every step, the forest grew thicker. The weather had changed in the blink of an eye. Dense clouds and the trees' crowded crowns choked out the light, turning day into night. Branches creaked and strained in the quickening wind.

Harper's legs and hands ached. She trusted the huskies to protect her from predators, but their incessant yowling caused her stomach to cramp with nerves.

"Kat," she called. "Kat, I think we should turn back."

She yelled twice more and louder without any response. She began to feel quite desperate. What if the Wish List gang had snatched Kat and Matty too?

Then Kat shouted, "Harper! Harper, hurry. We've found something."

The huskies began to whine and pull again. Harper could no longer contain them. Swept along in their wake, she was like a water-skier being towed by three different boats, all swerving in different directions. In the confusion, Thunder's leash slipped from her grasp. As Harper bent to try to catch it, Rebel spotted a delicious forest creature.

With a howl of delight, he and Dancer raced off in pursuit, followed by Rebel. Harper screamed their names, knowing it was hopeless. Camouflaged by their white and gray fur, the three huskies were as invisible as spirits amid the silver trunks of the birch.

Harper gave up the chase. Finding Riley was the priority. Kat could use her husky-whispering skills to round the escapees up later.

She ran in the direction she'd last heard Kat's voice, the snow squeaking beneath her boots. Witches' hair thornbushes snagged at her jacket. Without the huskies, she felt as exposed as a limping zebra on a plain full of lions.

A stitch stabbed at her side. She was slipping and sliding and ready to weep with exhaustion when she almost tripped over Matty's leash. Kat had looped it over a branch.

"She was here, Harper. Riley was here."

Kat brushed a tear from her cheek but didn't look around. She was crouched at the entrance of a crudely assembled but effective shelter of sticks and packed snow. At least three sets of boot prints—two large and one small—scuffed the surrounding ground.

Harper swallowed. "Where do you think she is now?"

Somewhere in the forest, the huskies started howling. Matty yelped, twisted free of the branch, and tore away, leash trailing. Kat barely noticed.

Wordlessly, she led Harper through the trees,

following the indents of footprints visible in the gloom. They ended at a track scarred by recent tire tracks.

"Maybe the rescue team found her and she's safe," Harper said hopefully.

Kat kicked at a stone. "Maybe the kidnappers found her and she's not."

BEAR SPIRIT

HARPER WRAPPED HER SCARF AROUND her face and jogged on the spot in a vain attempt to combat the skin-shredding wind. "Bet you anything that while we're out here getting pneumonia, those husky menaces are on the steps of our cabin, howling to get in."

"You're p-probably ri-r-right." Kat's teeth chattered so hard she could hardly get the words out. "I'm hoarse from calling for them. In any c-case, they have a better chance of surviving Storm Mindy than we do. Let's turn back."

"I think that might be best. I'm starting to hallucinate about saunas. It's that way, yeah?"

Kat fought down a wave of panic. She'd been sure it was the opposite direction. The trunks of the white birch offered no clues. The words of the woman in the bookshop kept running through her mind: *Three steps off the trail in the wrong direction can turn a stroll in the woods into a major search-and-rescue mission. Blink and a person's gone.*

Now you see them; now you don't.

Kat had resolved never to stray so much as a millimeter off any path in the Adirondacks and yet here she was, blundering blindly through the wilderness with no survival gear or compass, as helpless as any hapless hiker in the park's history.

"Harper, w-where's your phone? If there's a signal, maybe we should dial nine-one-one. If we can't find shelter, we . . . Harper, what's up? You look ill. Are you feeling faint? Is there any numbness in your fingers and toes? Harper, you're scaring me."

Her best friend was doing an Oscar-worthy impression of a goldfish flung from its bowl. Her unblinking stare shifted to something beyond Kat's left ear.

Kat smelled the black bear before she saw it. Its wildness thrilled her; terror paralyzed her. When it reared up and clacked its yellow teeth, her bones seemed to liquefy, and it took a superhuman effort of will not to curl up in a ball of fear in the snow.

Stand tall, Jet had advised, forgetting he was talking to two children. Clinging to each other was the most they could manage.

The bear appeared singularly unimpressed by their

lack of height or width. It moaned and swayed on immense paws with curling claws. It blew furious breaths.

"Don't suppose you have any bear-whispering techniques up your sleeve?" shouted Harper, recalling Jet's instruction about making lots of noise.

"Not a single one." Kat tried bellowing the words, but all that came out was a squeak.

There was a white patch on the bear's shoulder, the legacy of a wound so traumatic that the fur had never recovered. Kat wondered if a bullet had caused it and whether the shell was still embedded in its flesh or splintered bone. A lifetime of agony might explain the hatred blazing in its eyes.

Snow began to fall, lending magic to their lonely drama. Before the girls could get it together to *back away very, very slowly*, an icy gust of wind pinged them with grit and frosty leaves. A falling pine cone, transformed into a missile, startled the bear with a blow to the snout.

Without warning, it charged. Kat's vision filled with fur, fangs, and claws.

Every instinct will scream at you to sprint for your life, Jet had counseled. *Resist it. Your life depends on you doing the opposite.*

Out of the whirling snow came the four huskies. They intercepted the bear as it pounded toward the girls, causing it to skid to a halt and lash out at the dogs. The snow was coming down hard and it looked momentarily undecided about whether to continue the fight.

"Run!" screamed Harper.

Kat and the huskies fled too.

There is a time and a place for theoretical advice, but they weren't about to argue with a six-hundred-pound bear.

NINE LIVES

"NEVER AGAIN," SAID HARPER FROM THE depths of the sofa, pressing a palm to her forehead in the manner of a Victorian heroine taken poorly after a country walk. A bone-thawing soak in a bubble bath aside, she'd been horizontal on the cushions since their return.

"Never, ever again," she added for good measure. "For the next forty-eight hours, I refuse to set one foot outside of this cabin unless the roof is on fire or there's a nuclear war. If the Dog House—that's what I'm naming this place—is still standing after Storm Mindy's finished pounding it, we can text our parents and beg them to collect us by limo and transport us to a five-star hotel in New York City. I am so done with the wilderness. Do not even show me an ant."

Kat didn't blame her. There were only so many

near-death experiences a person could stand in one week without feeling overwhelmed. When she thought about the tree branch that had almost crushed them in Jet's truck, the runaway "toboggan," the near-bear attack, and the blizzard they'd stumbled through afterward, it did chill her blood just a little.

It was almost as if she had nine lives, like a cat. Cowering before the bear just a few hours earlier, Kat had been sure that if she made one false move, her current life would be over.

But it wasn't over. Nor, for all her protestations, was Harper's. Their lives were richer, and they were braver. Thanks to the heroism of the huskies, they'd survived to tell the tale. Kat knew she'd never forget the majesty of the black bear as it reared to its full height in the forest. It had worn its wildness like a cloak.

With snowflakes drifting all around it, the creature had seemed almost enchanted: a spirit bear from another world. Then it had attacked and become a monster. Now in Kat's mind it was something in between: a wild, free creature deserving of respect.

It wasn't only the bear that had had a fairy-tale aura about it that day. Guiding the girls home through the blinding snow, Thunder, Rebel, Matty, and Dancer had flanked them so closely that Kat had felt hugged; a valued member of their precious pack. The huskies' body warmth and loyalty had kept her going when all she wanted to do was give up. Without them, she and Harper would not have made it back to the cabin, of that Kat was horribly certain.

They'd clawed their way indoors in the nick of time. The big question now was whether the Dog House was built to withstand a storm like Mindy. The whole cabin shook, rattled, and strained under the force of the gale. The lake and mountain had been erased.

Even the huskies were glad to be indoors. They'd saved the girls' lives, but in a way, Kat and Harper had saved the huskies' lives first. Their kennels offered minimal shelter. Left alone in the storm without food, water, or extra blankets, the dogs wouldn't have lasted the night.

Instead, they were safely inside and loving it. On the sofa, Harper was laughing as Dancer and Rebel scrambled up to snuggle her. "I get the feeling the huskies have adopted us. Whether we like it or not, we're their family now."

"Yes, we are," said Kat, feeling a rush of affection for their furry friends. "We belong to them, and they belong to us."

She squeezed between Nomad and Fleet on the other sofa. "Harper, what we did today was stupidly risky and selfish and it could have ended—*nearly did end*—everything. But I don't regret it. We did what we did to try to save Riley."

"I don't regret it either," said Harper. "Not one bit."

Reluctantly, she reached for the TV remote. "Shall we do it?"

"We have to. Not knowing is worse."

They didn't need to wait long. Riley Matthews was headline news.

A now familiar newsreader said, "Daylesford Bank chairman Wainwright Matthews has posted a one-million-dollar reward for information leading to the safe return of his twelve-year-old daughter, Riley Gabriella, missing in the Adirondacks since early this morning.

"There are growing fears that Riley, star witness in the upcoming trial of alleged Wish List gangster Gerry Meeks, has been abducted. Riley's protection officers, who were both wounded in the ambush, remain critically ill and under armed guard in the ICU at an undisclosed hospital. Detectives hoping to glean some answers on the ambush are likely to face a long wait.

"Search-and-rescue efforts have also been hampered by Storm Mindy, which has brought whiteout conditions to the northern Adirondacks. With emergency services stretched to capacity and many roads impassable, detectives are concentrating their efforts on trying to track down Meeks's unidentified accomplices. Progress has been slow due to the number of copycat Wish List crimes—"

Harper muted the TV. "The good news is, so far as anyone can tell, Riley's still alive."

"The bad news is, she's probably in the clutches of vengeful Wish List villains," Kat said emotionally. "How can the police have failed so spectacularly to find Riley when somebody else obviously did? Why can't they identify the other members of the gang? Nine heists and their only suspect is a ninety-one-year-old. It's pathetic."

"If only I had my laptop," fumed Harper for the hundredth time. "We could show those plodding gumshoes a thing or two about solving mysteries."

"How would a laptop save Riley?" asked Kat. "What use is it as a crime-fighting device without the internet?"

Harper stared at her in mystification. "Among other things, it has Excel. I could have set up a spreadsheet to organize our clues. Without a laptop, I'm like a musician without an instrument, a dancer without a stage, a champion jockey without a racehorse, a—"

"I get it," sighed Kat. "But you could always use a pencil and paper."

"That's only one step up from dipping a porcupine quill in blood and berry juice and drawing wildebeests on a cave wall," Harper said melodramatically.

Kat threw up her hands. "Then I can't help you. I'm going to bake an apple crumble. Some of us don't need a laptop to organize our clues. We can use our brains."

NICE AS PIE

"LET'S START WITH WHAT WE KNOW," SAID
Harper, using a red Sharpie to write *THE CASE OF
THE MISSING STAR WITNESS* in bold across the top
of Kat's watercolor pad. Even she had to agree that scarlet
ink on hand-milled cotton board was several steps up
from a bloodied quill in a musty cave.

"Our best hope of finding Riley is to do what other
detectives haven't: identify the members of the gang.
That's if they're the ones who've got her. There are other
possible motives for a kidnapping—e.g., Riley's bank
chairman father. But for now, let's assume the Wish
Listers have her. Once we've done that, we need to figure
out where they could be hiding her."

"That's what I'm worried about," said Kat, rubbing
flour, oats, and oil between her palms to make the apple

crumble topping. Nomad sat at her feet, nibbling the scraps. "American geography is *not* my strong point."

"You're forgetting Storm Mindy."

Kat raised a floury eyebrow. "Not much chance of that. It's like a marching band's playing on the roof. Look out the window. It's as if nothing exists except snow and ice, you and me, six huskies, a raccoon . . . and four thousand bears."

Harper clutched her head. "Don't mention the bears. Not for a decade or two. Or ever. What I meant was, the weather might work in our favor. If the emergency services are stretched to capacity and some roads are impassable, the kidnappers might have decided to lie low in the Adirondacks till Mindy blows over."

"I hadn't thought of that. They might be snowed in and trapped, like us!" said Kat, cheering considerably.

"Yes, but we're in a race against time. Soon as the roads reopen and the High Peaks region is crawling with cops, they'll be gone like the wind. They'll either take Riley with them or they'll make her disappear in the Adirondacks."

It was a grim prospect, and when the television popped, they both jumped. On the screen, an image of a tropical island buckled and shrank to a dot before flickering back to normal.

"No!" cried Harper. "That's all we need. If Mindy knocks out communications, we could be cut off from the outside world. That would be a disaster, especially since no one knows we're here. Better text your mom and tell her we're okay while you can."

Kat didn't hesitate. Wiping her hands on a squirrel dish towel, she typed:

Hi Mom, hope you're not too lonely in Lake Placid. Storm Mindy's arrived but we're keeping busy. I'm baking the apple crumble you taught me and Harper's doing something mysterious and artistic with my watercolor pad. K & H xx

Her mother replied in an instant.

Darling, I'm proud of you both. Theo and I like to take credit for raising such resourceful daughters, but the truth is you and Harper are wonderful all on your own. Not a lot to do in snowy Lake Placid except laze around reading, eating, and having the occasional massage. Could be worse! Missing you very much. Keep out of the cold! Love Mum xx

Kat read the message twice. "Why do I get the feeling that she's secretly enjoying herself?"

"Maybe she is," said Harper. "That's okay, isn't it? We are too."

It was true. As long as Mirror Lake remained in the grip of Mindy's glacial jaws, the likelihood of the cabin's owner returning unexpectedly was minimal. The lane was under half a meter of snow at least. With no safe way of reaching Nightingale Lodge until the worst of the storm had passed, the girls had no choice but to relax. For now, the Dog House was home.

As a consequence, the living room was carpeted in huskies, chew toys, and cushion innards, and a snowdrift of flour coated the kitchen tiles. When Kat lifted the lid on the pot, the heavenly fragrance of stewed apple and cinnamon filled the air.

"What's this?" asked Harper, prodding a large cardboard box Kat had deposited on the armchair.

"I found it in the cupboard under the stairs. It's full of games."

Harper opened it eagerly and was crestfallen to discover they were board games. She'd envisaged something more entertaining. A pinball machine, Ping-Pong, or an indoor bowling setup. "They should be called bored games. Monopoly and Snakes and Ladders have been around since Gerry Meeks was a baby. I do like Scrabble. That can stay. As for the jigsaw puzzles . . . Wait, what's this?"

She pulled a package from the bottom of the box. "Kat Wolfe, you're a legend."

"Can I have that in writing?" kidded Kat, who was in the kitchen putting the finishing touches to the crumble.

"After the rattlesnake story, I was starting to have doubts about our friendship . . ."

"Hold on! Two seconds ago, I was a legend."

Harper grinned. "Now you're forgiven even that gruesome tale. From this day on, I owe you forever times infinity because somehow, in this cabin at the end of the universe, in the land that time forgot, you've uncovered a brand-new, still sealed Raspberry Pi."

Kat was confused. "There's a raspberry pie in the game box?"

"Not an edible pie, a *Raspberry Pi*. Don't tell me you've never heard of them. They're dead-cheap, dead-basic kit computers, but if you're tech-savvy and add a few components, you can really make them fly."

"And you can build one?"

"In my sleep. I'll start right now. Time me. How long does it take to bake an apple crumble?"

"Thirty minutes. You can assemble a Pi as quick as that?"

"Just watch me."

ROCKY ROAD

THAT NIGHT, HARPER DREAMED SHE WAS
in a snowbound wilderness theme park. Carnival music
thudded relentlessly. Every loop of the roller coaster
carried her nearer to a den of pacing bears. She begged
the operator to stop the ride, but no matter how loudly
she shouted, he didn't seem to hear her. He just stared
ahead with a fixed grin.

"Why won't you listen?" she sobbed.

"Harper, listen!"

The scene wobbled and was gone. She opened her
eyes to darkness as black as velvet. Kat was leaning
over her, saying something. Harper tried groggily to
comprehend what it was.

Downstairs, the huskies appeared to be using the
living room as a practice run for a sled race. They were

husky "talking" nonstop and knocking over chairs. Something smashed. A bell tinkled.

Adrenaline kicked Harper into life.

"The owner's come home!" She fumbled for her glasses on the bedside table.

"Or it could be robbers," whispered Kat. "Or the police. Whichever, we're in trouble."

They reached for the lamp at the same time, knocking it over. It hit the ground with a crack and broke.

Gripping hands, the girls huddled against the wall, as if that would make whatever was happening go away. They waited for footsteps. None came.

Instead, there was a burst of howling followed by a distinct: *Whoop-whoop. Whoop-whoop. Whoop-whoop. Hisssss.*

"Rocky!" Harper exclaimed. "Oh my goodness, if we don't get down there fast, he'll be a raccoon canapé for six huskies."

Kat flew to turn on the main light, but the electricity was out.

"The fuse might have blown," said Harper. "I think I saw a flashlight in the chest of drawers."

Falling over the suitcase and bumping into a chair added more bruises to Kat's already impressive collection before she found it. The yellow beam illuminated their untidy space. Harper was sitting on her bed, her black bob mussed up, her pajama top buttoned crookedly.

They took the stairs in action-hero bounds, Kat still clutching the torch. When they burst into the living room, the huskies froze in place like museum waxworks, their expressions ranging from guilty to unapologetically mischievous.

Dancer was on her hind legs in the kitchen, her paws reaching almost to the top of the refrigerator door. Brave Rocky was shooting her a death glare from up high, like a lone knight under siege in a castle turret.

Kat was no raccoon expert, but she did know that they were intelligent, sociable, and capable of more than fifty different vocalizations. Cornered, Rocky whistled, snarled, whinnied, grunted, and growled like a one-raccoon orchestra.

Two words from Kat and the huskies slunk out of the kitchen. Dancer was the last to leave, casting a wounded *How dare you spoil my fun?* look at her as she went.

"If you keep an eye on the huskies, Harper, I'll try to calm Rocky. He must be hungry or else he wouldn't have risked the wrath of six huskies. I'd like to try to feed him something before he goes back to his den."

As Kat spoke soothingly to the raccoon, Harper went to turn on the lights. None worked. Her phone had no signal. Though it was plugged in, the battery was flat. The TV was dead too.

"Kat, remember how on our first night you said it was as if aliens had abducted everyone and we were the only people left in the world? I think it might actually have happened."

Absorbed in opening a can of peaches for the raccoon, Kat laughed but didn't look around.

"I'm serious," said Harper. "Not about the aliens, but about feeling that we're the only ones left alive. We're cut off from everyone and everything. And the scary part is not one person on the entire planet knows we're here. We might as well be marooned on an ice floe in Alaska."

Now she had Kat's full attention. "Jet drove us here, so at least he can give his aunt the address if anything really bad happens to us—which it won't. How long do you reckon it'll be before the power's restored?"

"Who knows? In history, we learned about an ice storm in Washington and Idaho that knocked out power for a couple of weeks, but I doubt that would happen now."

"I don't care about the electricity," said Kat. "We have candles, a fire, and a gas stove. Storm Mindy won't last forever. I do care about Riley. If we can't watch the news and we don't have Wi-Fi, how will we know if she's been rescued?"

A piercing *whoop-whoop* was their one-second warning before pandemonium erupted again. Unnoticed by the girls, Dancer had sneaked back into the kitchen.

She jumped as high as she could, trying to reach the raccoon. Squealing and mewling, Rocky took evasive action, but Dancer managed to nip him before Kat could grab her collar.

The raccoon shot behind the cabinet and was gone.

"Phew, that was a lucky escape," said Harper, shaken.

"It wasn't lucky for Rocky," said Kat, indicating a smear of blood on the tiles. "Looks as if he's wounded. Wherever he's taken refuge, we need to find him."

SNOWMAGEDDON

"WE'VE DONE A LOT OF MAD THINGS, BUT this has to be the maddest," said Harper as they inched their way along a rope that they'd secured to the porch railings. "It's Snowmaggedon out here. What if one of us breaks a limb or catches pneumonia? We can't exactly call for help. How do we get to the emergency room—by husky sled? Oh, I forgot. We don't have one."

"Yes, but it's *our* fault that Rocky was bitten." Kat raised her voice to compete with the wailing wind. "There was always a chance he'd come back. We should have created a safe area for him. He must have got the shock of his life to find six huskies lying in wait. Now he's bleeding. He might need stitches or an antibiotic." She turned away, shouting over her shoulder, "Go be in the warm Dog House if that's what you want. I'm going to find Rocky."

"Okay, okay," grizzled Harper as spiky shards of ice needled her cheeks. "Kat, wait. I promise we won't give up till you're one hundred percent satisfied that he's the happiest, healthiest raccoon in all the Adirondacks. But maybe there's a better way."

"What better way?"

For all her fighting talk, Kat was ready to consider all options. The chef at the Full-Belly Deli had been talking from experience when he warned them about winter in the wilderness. She no longer doubted that a person could freeze to death in their own backyard.

"We're detectives," said Harper, steering Kat beneath the shelter of the porch. "Let's use detective techniques to track Rocky down. When you saw him up close, was his fur wet? Did he look bedraggled?"

"Not at all."

"Trust me, if Rocky was outside in this beast of a storm for even five minutes, he'd have looked like a raccoon Popsicle. I think his den is indoors."

Kat, who was rapidly turning into a Kat Popsicle, was sufficiently interested in Harper's theory to allow herself to be led back into the cabin. There, they evicted two huskies from the hearth and unthawed their hands over the flames.

"Say you're right and Rocky's den *is* in the Dog House," said Kat. "Any idea where it might be? We've explored every corner of it. We've unlocked every door, opened every cupboard."

As she spoke, she felt an unpleasant prickle of conscience. Sooner or later, the storm would be over and the cabin's owner would come roaring up the drive. There'd be a reckoning. Her mum and Harper's dad would go berserk once they learned the truth and saw the state of the Dog House. They could be sued. Kat was not looking forward to it.

"You read more mysteries than I do," Harper was saying. "When the detective stumbles across secret passages or hidden rooms, where are they generally located?"

"Behind bookcases," Kat answered at once. "Or under floorboards or rugs."

"We can rule out this room or the kitchen because the huskies would have sniffed out any raccoon den days ago. And there can't be a secret passage behind the bookcase on the top floor because the shower's on the other side of the wall."

"Also, I keep tripping over the rug in our room," said Kat. "So I can tell you for sure that there's nothing hidden under there. And the front of the cabin is on stilts, so there's nothing under there."

Their eyes met. There was only one other possibility.

They flew to the door that led to the main bedroom with such enthusiasm that Kat skidded in her socks and almost did need to be stretchered off to the ER.

It was the only bit of the cabin that they and the huskies hadn't managed to destroy. The geometric rug at the foot of the bed was pristine. Harper lifted it with the flourish of a stagehand raising a theater curtain.

The trapdoor beneath wasn't even locked.

"Before, when I said you were a genius, I didn't mean it," said Kat.

"Thanks . . . ?"

"Now I do."

They descended the steps with extreme trepidation, frightened of what they might find.

"What if the owner has been here all along—frozen into a statue in the basement?" said Harper when they were halfway down. "Could be a whole family."

Kat's head filled with images of skeletons sagging amid piles of moth-eaten clothes, rusty bikes, or three-legged Adirondack chairs. If she hadn't been so anxious about Rocky, she'd have refused to go on.

The first surprise was that the light flickered on. "Must be solar or be powered by some external source," said Harper. "Why else would this light work and the rest of the place be in darkness?"

The second surprise was that a husky racing sled was parked on the gleaming linoleum floor of a large storeroom. Harnesses, snow boots, and other husky equipment was stacked nearby or hung neatly on hooks. Kat realized now that the snow-covered trellis they'd glimpsed when they walked back from the kennels must have disguised the garage-type door, cut into the side of the hill.

At the back of the storeroom was a dog bed and water and food bowls—both empty. Curled up in the bed, looking dejected but unafraid, was the raccoon.

Kat realized immediately that she'd been mistaken about his wilderness den. "He's somebody's pet," she said, picking him up and cradling him in her arms. "Probably an orphan. Look, there's the doggy door so he can go outside, and there's the pipe he uses to climb to the kitchen. He must have been so frightened and hungry when his rescuer didn't come home."

While Kat examined Rocky for cuts and abrasions, Harper took a look around. She tried the door of a tall steel cabinet and gave a low whistle.

"Whoever lives here is a prepper."

"What's a prepper?"

"Someone who believes in preparing for worst-case scenarios like a war or a natural disaster. They're survivalists. They tend to believe that if there's a super volcano, say, and things fall apart, everyone's on their own. They don't depend on the government."

"We are on our own," said Kat. "And nobody from the government has come to help us. What do you need to be a prepper?"

Harper waved an arm. "This stuff. Cans of lentils,

beans, carrots, and tomatoes. Massive bags of rice and pasta. Waterproof matches. Flints to start fires. Water purifiers. Space blankets. A tent, a sleeping bag, and a camping stove. Solar panels. Oh, goody, there are wind-up flashlights and lamps. Candles too. Let's take everything upstairs."

Kat put down Rocky. He'd suffered a minor nip but was otherwise unharmed. "Pass me the first aid kit." She unzipped the bulging bag. "This is ten times better than mine. Antibiotics, dressings, painkillers, and Steri-Strips. They're used for stitching wounds. A scalpel too. Who needs a doctor? What have you found?"

Harper was wrestling a heavy black case from the bottom shelf. She hesitated for a moment, hands trembling, before popping the silver catches. "Forget what I said about the cabin being cursed. I'm starting to think it's my dream house. This, dear Kat, is an Earth2Sky 4800 portable satellite terminal. It'll connect to the internet in under sixty seconds whether you're on the Southern Ocean or the summit of Everest. Works off a car battery as well, so electricity is optional."

"Are you saying what I think you're saying?"

"I'm saying that if we want to find Riley, this is our best shot."

THE WRONG WRITERS

FUELED BY THE HONEY-AND-COCONUT granola they'd discovered in the cellar, the girls set to work at once. They'd made a little progress after Harper set up the Raspberry Pi the previous night. Now, as she put it, they were "jet-propelled."

"Riley won't be sleeping, so neither should we," she said. "We're racing the clock. With every passing minute, the danger that the kidnappers will get rid of her just to shut her up or because she's no longer useful increases."

"Also, if everything goes smoothly with your dad's flight and my mum's car rental, they'll be cruising up the drive of Nightingale Lodge on Thursday afternoon," Kat reminded her. "That's tomorrow. Approximately thirty-six hours from now."

"No pressure, then," said Harper. "All we have to do is pack up our stuff, clean the Dog House from top to bottom, mosey around the lake, and move into our other cabin. I'm longing to see them, but once the adults show up, our search for Riley is over."

Kat was 99 percent sure she was right. Her mum and Professor Lamb were kind, reasonable people. They'd say in their kind, reasonable way, *Girls, you have to trust that the police are pulling out all the stops to save Riley. The professionals will find her, you'll see.*

They'd never believe that Kat and Harper—bear-spray-forgetting strangers to the Adirondacks wilderness—could succeed at finding Riley when local detectives and search-and-rescue teams had failed.

Harper was at the window. "It's so still and silent outside. Storm Mindy must have peaked. Soon she'll be moving on."

Kat wasn't convinced. Ten minutes earlier, she'd taken two of the huskies outside. The cold was so extreme that she'd wrapped her scarf around her face and peered through the stitches lest her eyeballs turn to sorbet. The only positive was that the wind had died down. Nothing ruffled the huskies' thick silver fur.

Even so, there was something crouched about the weather, as if Storm Mindy were a snow leopard, not a wolf. Her claws were sheathed for now. Kat didn't trust her not to lash out.

In the Dog House, Harper stationed herself at one

end of the dining room table with the Raspberry Pi she'd built and boosted with added bits and pieces. The Earth2Sky satellite terminal wasn't the only gadget she'd discovered in the storeroom.

Kat had been impressed when Harper had managed to power up the satellite and get online in under a minute, but the real magic was watching her turn the cheap and dinky laptop into a flying machine that met her high standards.

Harper polished her glasses and flexed her fingers.

Kat giggled. Her best friend was like a pajama-clad jockey at the starting gates at Ascot Racecourse. She could almost hear the commentary: *Champion rider Harper Lamb is balanced low over Raspberry Pi's withers, ready to explode onto the track . . .*

Kat sat at the other end of the table with her low-tech watercolor pad and red Sharpie, plus a pile of yellowing newspapers she'd found in the garage.

Harper tapped the laptop keys experimentally. "Ready, Kat? You practice your old-fashioned detective methods and I'll use my twenty-first-century detective methods, and we'll see who wins."

"We win when we rescue Riley," said Kat.

Strong emotion rippled through Harper. She'd been so focused on creating the fastest machine possible for their detective task force that she'd temporarily forgotten that they were trying to save a living, breathing, terrified girl. She blinked away a tear.

"We win when we rescue Riley," she agreed.

Before anything else, they checked that Riley did in fact still need rescuing. There was no point in beginning any investigation, twenty-first-century or otherwise, if the American girl had been plucked from the snow by a search team and bundled away to a hospital or her father's penthouse since they'd last watched the TV the previous afternoon.

Riley was still missing.

Photos of a haggard Wainwright Matthews plastered local and social media. The only news was that there was no news. The twin rewards—$1 million for information leading to Riley's safe return, and $1 million for information leading to the recovery of the diamond necklace—had flooded police hotlines with hoax calls.

In the words of one detective, they were struggling to "sort out the jokers" as they sifted through possible sightings.

Storm Mindy had strained resources further as police and emergency workers dealt with record numbers of traffic accidents, power outages, and snow-related injuries. Kat had the impression that while Riley's case was important to the cops, it was not the priority.

There was something unsettling about being online again. Even Harper found it disconcerting, as bleak or gaudy images of pop stars, award ceremonies, vicious politicians, wars, and natural disasters streamed into their wilderness cabin. She had to fight the temptation to slam the lid on them.

"Now we have Wi-Fi, we could video-call your mum and my dad and say hi," she told Kat, who was reading a news story over her shoulder. "If you want to, that is."

Kat stiffened. "It's nice to know we can, but they'll be sleeping. Let's think about it later in the day."

Harper was equally hesitant and not just because of the time. As soon as they opened a connection to their parents, their investigation was over.

"What about asking one of our deputies to do some research for us?" asked Kat. "Edith, Kai, or maybe even Jasper?"

Jasper was Harper's father-approved mentor when it came to hacking. A former student of Professor Lamb's at Yale University in Connecticut, he was often called upon to help the FBI. He'd lent Kat and Harper a hand on their first-ever case.

Harper shook her head. "If Dad gets the smallest hint that I've been online on our vacation, I'll be toast. Kai was so brilliant on our last case, he would have been perfect, but he's in China with his dad. Too bad that he's on a screen ban too."

"Looks as if we're on our own, then," said Kat, returning to her end of the table.

"That's all right," said Harper. "I kind of prefer it that way."

She brought up the website of the Royal Manhattan. "If you make notes on what we know so far, I'll attempt to hack the hotel website."

"Is that legal?"

"Legal schmegal," Harper said airily. "It's not like I'm after credit card details or people's private information. If the police haven't already taken it, I want the CCTV footage for the last couple of hours of the event on September twenty-seventh, the night the diamond necklace was stolen. We might be able to identify Gerry's accomplices—if he had any. If we crack the case, we'll be doing the hotel a favor. They'll thank us."

Her fingers flew as she tapped in computer code. "While I'm doing this, tell me more about Riley."

With those words, Kat was transported back to the forest. She could hear the loon's haunting call and see Riley as clearly as if she was sitting there with them. Her striking blue eyes and choppy, strawberry-blond hair. Her ready smile and bubbling laugh.

"Underneath, though, she seemed lonely and a bit

sad," she told Harper. "Now we know she was away from her family and with bodyguards, but it was more than that. She said she didn't have many friends—not real ones."

As she talked, Kat made notes on her pad. "She didn't mention a mum, only her father. He won't let her have a cat because of his allergies. She thought he might be making them up."

"I bet he'd give her a kitten in a heartbeat now, hay fever or no hay fever," said Harper. "The other night, on the news, he looked cold and supercilious. Now he looks destroyed."

She started typing again. "Go on. Anything else you remember?"

"Riley adores her nan, who's crazy about the environment and birds. I got the idea that Riley's dad was as allergic to her grandmother as he is to cats. Riley hadn't seen her for ages. She was proud that her nan had gone up against some company that leaked toxic metal into a lake near her house, making the loons sick and forgetful of their chicks."

"Did her grandmother win that battle?"

"She must have done. According to Riley, the toxic metal company were the sorriest people on earth once she'd finished with them."

Harper lifted both arms, like a boxer celebrating

a knockout. "Kat, I'm in! I'm prowling the hidden passages of the Royal Manhattan. Imagine spending millions on renovations and sparing no expense on a star-studded grand opening while saving every possible dime on internet security. What were they thinking? I'll leave them a friendly note. Remind them that they have a responsibility to protect the data of their guests."

In the time it took Kat to walk around the table, Harper had found the cache of CCTV videos.

"As I suspected. We're too late. The tape for the week of the September event is missing. The cops must have it. Doesn't matter. There would have been a zillion photos taken that night. We won't be able to download the official ones, but . . . Ah, here are some taken by the assistant manager. He has a desperate case of the camera shakes, but they're better than nothing. There's a printer downstairs. We can print them out later."

"Harper!"

"Do you want to find Riley or not? Over to you, Kat. What do we know about Gerry Meeks and his gang of merry thieves?"

"Only his age and that he's a retired insurance salesman. Didn't you say that the director of Shady Oaks mentioned that his granddaughter had died? As far as we know, he's alone in the world. Before his arrest, he enjoyed reading mysteries and doing yoga in his room.

He supposedly beat everyone at chess. That's it. That's all we know."

"We also know that he snatched an heiress's diamond necklace, while she was wearing it and in a crowded ballroom," said Harper. "That's quite a brazen move for an old guy."

Kat glanced up from her notebook. "Don't forget there were a whole series of diversions that night. There were climate-change activists with blowtorches, lobsters being liberated from their tanks, and the fire across the street. The Force Ten security guards who were supposed to be keeping watch over the necklace were helping put out the blaze."

"Thanks for the reminder, Detective Wolfe. If the fire was also a diversion, that could mean it was started deliberately."

"Good thinking, Detective Lamb!" said Kat, making a note on her pad with the red Sharpie. "I'm working on the theory that there are at least five or six members of the Wish List gang."

"What makes you think that?"

Kat counted them off on her fingers. "Gerry Meeks, plus his three visitors, plus the man and woman who took Riley from the snow shelter we found. I'd say the man's boots were size eleven, so he must be tall. The other person was a small woman. That's if the Wish List gang were responsible for her disappearance."

Kat passed the list she'd made to Harper.

WISH LIST GANG

Gerry Meeks
Tall, elegant woman
Petite woman
Woman with thick, curly hair
Man with huge boots who took Riley from the snow
Female accomplice (may be a new person or the
    petite visitor)

"The curly-haired visitor could have been wearing a wig," observed Harper.

Kat made a note. "On paper, we don't have a lot to go on, but I'll start looking for patterns. The gang members might be linked by age, job, or geography. The items stolen might give us clues too."

Harper was back at her screen. "Before you start working on that, come watch me hack into the Shady Oaks website."

Kat was horrified. "Harper, you can't. That's an invasion of privacy. It'll be full of patients' medical details."

"I wouldn't dream of poking around in people's medical details. Anyway, I'll be in and out in five minutes. Shady Oaks is not the sort of place I'd want to linger. All I'm going to do is run a teensy-weensy search for Gerry's name in the director's emails. What was her name again? Ah, here we are: Sylvia Jarman."

She entered code faster than a pianist playing Rachmaninoff.

Kat held her breath. "Are you through their firewall?"

"'Course. Mainly because they didn't bother putting up a firewall. Told you it would be easy. One moment while I search . . . Here we go. Take a look at this."

```
To: sylvia.jarman@shadyoaks.com
From: staciebeggs@gmail.com
Date: September 30
Subject: Meeks Mail
Hi Sylv,
Boy were you having a crystal ball moment
when you asked me to take a sneak peek
for snail mail in Gerry's room while
you gave that cheeky young detective a
dressing-down over the search warrant.
Or lack of it!
    Gerry wrote a ton of letters and got
an avalanche back, but he must have had
a secret bonfire because I only found a
single page tossed in the trash. It was
a close-run thing. One of the maids came
in to empty the wastepaper basket just
as I was leaving. Anyhoo, I've attached
a scan of it here for your perusal.
```

It shows a deranged mind, if you ask me. The handwriting alone should get a person locked up. Who calls themselves a Wrong Writer and signs a letter with a number, not a name?

What's clearer than California is that our Gerry's been telling tales out of school about the meals and staff here. Makes me think we should censor all our residents' mail. Though it's tough to argue with the comment about our receptionist not having the sense God gave a canary!

That said, I hold my hand up to signing Gerry out with one of the women calling herself "A. Relative." She reminded me of the gardener's daughter. Remember that Italian man we had to manage out because he lacked communication skills? Despite the age gap, he and Gerry were as thick as thieves. Always chattering away in Italian and exchanging books—a constant source of mystery to me because Emilio could barely speak English. No, I lie. I suspect he spoke it perfectly, but it suited his contrary nature to pretend otherwise.

Did you know that Gerry spoke four languages? I can't imagine why. He had no passport and shuffled paper his whole life. I'm still trying to wrap my brain around his arrest. Quiet, dull Gerry lifting an heiress's $50 million diamond necklace WHILE SHE WAS WEARING IT!? You couldn't make it up. Then I got to thinking that maybe his very dullness was the clue we all missed. Ms. Stevenson in room 12 has a theory that he was a spy in World War II. Maybe she was onto something.

Back to the gardener's daughter. I only ever met her once, and I have no memory for faces, so don't take my word for it. There was just something about her attitude that reminded me of him.

Up to you whether you show the letter to the cops. If Detective WhatsHisFace gets his paws on it, he'll lock Gerry up and throw away the key. Who knows why Gerry did what he did, but he's always been kind to me. Personally, I'd

accidentally on purpose drop it in the
common-room fire.

Keep me posted on developments!

Stace x

Stacie Beggs

Senior Living Coordinator

Harper clicked on the attachment. A pale blue letter
popped up. Stacie was correct about one thing: the
handwriting was atrocious. The black ink was so illegible
that Kat and Harper skimmed the parts about the dire
meals and canary-brained receptionist and went directly
to the neatly printed section in different handwriting at
the end.

Dear G,

Here's your brief. Watch yourself but
don't be nervous. The Wrong Writers have
your back.

Date: September 27.

Pickup: SO at 3pm.

Operatives: Full House

Target: WL9, 11pm–11:45pm.

Degree of Difficulty: 11!!

Main Event: WW7RH 11pm–Midnight

Yours in Truth,

WW6

Harper closed the site and turned to Kat. "That clears up one thing. Whatever else Gerry Meeks is, innocent he's not."

Kat was rereading the note. "The media nicknamed them the Wish List gang, but maybe they really call themselves the Wrong Writers. WW6 could stand for Wrong Writer Six. There's also a Wrong Writer Seven. Do you think that means there are seven members of the gang?"

"The Wrong Writers sounds more like a creative-writing group for failed novelists," said Harper. "Maybe that's what they have in common. They're stealing stuff for extra cash so they can write bestsellers in the lap of luxury."

An internet search returned nothing but writing tips. Harper yawned. "I'm going to take a break and make a hot chocolate. Want one?"

Kat nodded vaguely. She kept looking at the words she had written on her pad. *Watch yourself but don't be nervous. The Wrong Writers have your back.*

She'd heard the phrase before, she was sure of it. All she had to do was figure out where.

THE CLUE CLUB

IT WAS A SHOCK TO SEE RILEY'S FACE again.

Yes, they'd seen her on the news, but there was something about physically holding the photo Harper had printed out that made Kat feel as if Riley were in the room with them. It lent urgency to their quest and made Riley flesh and blood again.

It wasn't a posed picture, and Riley wasn't smiling. The assistant hotel manager's shaky camerawork had blurred her features. She was a small, out-of-place figure glimpsed behind a gaggle of glamorous celebrities who collectively displayed more teeth than a great white as they grinned at someone out of shot.

Though Riley's face was washed-out by the low-on-ink printer, the disbelief on it was unmistakable. Her mouth was slightly open, and she was staring in the opposite direction from everyone else.

Gerry Meeks wasn't visible. Nor was Cynthia Hollinghurst or her diamond necklace. But the time stamp (11:06 P.M.) on the photo and Riley's appalled expression were enough to make them 99 percent certain that the snapshot had captured the robbery.

Encouraged by their progress, the girls redoubled their efforts to identify the gang members.

"We don't have time for absolute proof," said Harper. "Wild guesses are fine. Any outlandish hypothesis will do."

Kat was one step ahead of her on the wild guesses and outlandish hypotheses.

She'd already added the Italian gardener and his daughter to the list of possible gangsters, because there was no evidence that Gerry had other friends at Shady Oaks.

"Who'd blame Emilio for pretending he couldn't speak English when Stacie Beggs was around?" commented Harper. "If she's anything like her emails, she's deeply annoying."

Emilio's surname had been in a gardening newsletter on the Shady Oaks website. From there, Harper had tracked him to a park in her hometown, West Hartford, Connecticut, where an Emilio D'Angelo was head gardener. A short bio on the park's blog mentioned his daughter, Bianca, an artist based in Napa Valley, California.

"California's on the west coast of the United States, and New Jersey's on the east," said Harper, hopping onto Bianca D'Angelo's Instagram page. "The chances of her swinging by Shady Oaks to take Gerry on an outing are pretty slim."

"She might have only done it once," countered Kat. "One of Gerry's visitors was described as long-limbed and elegant. That sums up Bianca."

Kat leaned closer to Harper's screen. "Wait, go back. See that photo of her smiling outside a jazz bar in New Orleans? The painting the gang stole came from a New Orleans gallery. I'm putting Bianca down as an art thief."

Harper laughed. "What happened to people being innocent until proven guilty?"

"If we're going to save Riley, we don't have the luxury of giving them the benefit of the doubt," Kat told her. "For the next thirty-six hours, they're all guilty until proven innocent."

"Eek! You might be right."

Harper was staring at a page from Bianca's high school yearbook. "Is that a mullet on her head? I'm amazed she wasn't arrested for crimes against hair. She did get it styled for the prom, though. What a difference. Don't she and her football player boyfriend look cute all dressed up?"

She squinted at the tiny photo. "Hmm, there's

something familiar about him. I wonder why. Oh, here's Bianca's yearbook list.

BIANCA D'ANGELO

Voted Girl Most Likely to: Save a Rain Forest or Become the Next Agatha Christie

Best Friend: My sister, Elena

Dating: Rob!

Hobbies: Oil painting, Reading, and Creative Writing

Goals: Turning My Hobbies into a Career That Pays the Rent!

Heroes: Frida Kahlo (artist) and Antonio Camilleri (author)

"Ever heard of Antonio Camilleri?"

"I think he's an Italian mystery writer," said Kat. "There's a TV series based on his books. I've watched one or two with my mum. You could be right about the gang members being failed novelists. So far, they seem to have books in common."

Harper was scrolling down the page. "Oh no! Bianca's sister died from cancer two years after they left high school. Bianca and Emilio must have been devastated."

"That's horrible. I wonder if Bianca moved to California to get away from the memories. Did she marry the football player?"

"No, but they stayed close. There's a photo of her hugging him in the hospital and another of him playing guitar in a band called the Three Chords."

The temperature had dipped dramatically in the cabin. Kat went to put another log on the fire while Harper kept scrolling.

"Does the band have a website?"

"A one-pager. Guess they didn't hit the big time. They split up a couple of years ago . . . Oh, wow. *Now* I know why Rob's so familiar."

"Why? Why?"

Kat rushed over to look at the screen.

"He was one of the Lautner brothers. Years ago, when Dad and I were still living in Connecticut, Rob and Michael Lautner were college football stars and local heroes."

"Are we talking British football or American football?"

"We're talking about what Americans call football, not what you Brits call football and we call soccer," said Harper with a grin. "Michael got some minor injury early on and quit, but Rob was on track to be a superstar. He was signed by one of the top NFL teams. Everyone was so happy for him. But before he could sign the contract, he got called up by the U.S. Army Reserve and sent to Iraq."

Kat gave her an anxious look. "Please don't tell me he was wounded in Iraq and could never play football again."

"No, he came home without a scratch. But days later, he was knocked off his motorbike and lost both his lower legs. I remember the headlines. The whole town went into mourning."

Kat felt quite depressed on Rob's behalf. "Then he can't possibly be a Wish List gang member. No one would turn to crime after a tragedy like that."

Harper was speed-reading a magazine article about Rob. "Hmm, I wouldn't rule him out just yet. Rob might have changed and become bitter after his dream died. Hey, hold on—he's married to a nurse now: Kiara Thompson. Credits her with saving his life. They share a passion for books and she's into oriental art . . . What if he stole the Ming vase to thank her for taking care of him after his accident?"

"I suppose it's possible," said Kat. "Have you noticed how everything keeps circling back to books, though? Does the story say anything about Rob enjoying writing? Is he working on his memoirs?"

"Nah, but the reporter does ask him if his brother likes reading as much as he does."

"And does he?"

"Apparently, Michael's a trucker these days. A

long-distance semi driver. Rob says his brother is dyslexic and never took to reading but now loves listening to audiobooks as he drives."

Kat said slowly, "A trucker would be a good person to have around if you were planning heists across the country."

Harper shot her an admiring glance. "Yes, he sure would. Let's add Michael to our list. And check out this photo of Rob's wife. She has thick, curly hair, like one of Gerry's visitors. Coincidence or not? How's our gang looking now?"

Kat fetched her watercolor pad and filled in the gaps.

WISH LIST GANG?

Gerry Meeks—Retired Insurance Salesman,
   New Jersey
Emilio D'Angelo—Gardener, Connecticut
Bianca D'Angelo—Artist, California
Rob Lautner—Ex-Football Player, Saratoga, NY
Kiara Thompson—Nurse, Saratoga, NY
Michael Lautner—Lorry Driver, Everywhere, U.S.A.
Petite woman?

Pleased with their efforts, they took a break at around 10:00 A.M., working their way through a bag of chips and a jar of salsa. Rebel made puppy eyes at Kat, but she refused to share.

"Salt's bad for you," she informed the husky, "but if you keep being an angel for a little while longer, I'll give you an early dinner."

She passed the bag to Harper. "I can't believe how much we've found out. Do people realize how much of their lives are online?"

"Some do, some don't." Harper shrugged. "Some just don't care."

She did internet searches with one hand while eating chips with the other. "Hey, it turns out that Rob Lautner's a personal trainer in Saratoga these days. Works with disabled athletes and veterans. An all-around good guy—supposedly."

"Everyone in our wild-guess gang is supposedly nice," said Kat. "Or at least they were before they became America's Most Wanted Robbers. Something catastrophic must have happened to turn them wicked. Have you found out any more about Gerry's past? Maybe he really was a spy."

"He's been retired for thirty years, so I doubt there'll be much online, but I'll take a look."

There were scores of stories on Gerry Meeks's arrest, but only one mention of his former life in an insurance forum.

"They should market this as a cure for insomnia," Harper said, scrolling through page after page of turgid discussions about premium increases and fake insurance claims.

Eventually, she found Gerry's name in a chat between two insurance workers.

Best investigator I ever met was Gerry Meeks. Retired last year. Specialized in high-dollar fraud. Our boss pretty much broke down and cried when he left. His whole career, Gerry only ever lost one case.

Which case was that?

I'd tell you, but I'd have to kill you after! I will tell ya that if anyone deserved a cushy retirement, Meeks did. After his granddaughter died, tho, I heard the life went out of him. Emily was his whole world. Speaking of grandkids, want to get together for a family BBQ and some tennis sometime?

"An insurance *investigator*?" Kat tried to reconcile the image of a dashing James Bond type with the frail man who'd stumbled into the courthouse. "The *best* investigator. So not just a paper pusher after all."

"This casts a whole new light on things," said Harper. "With Emily gone and nothing to lose, did Gerry decide to help himself to a piece of high-dollar pie?"

"See if you can find anything on that case he lost."

Harper couldn't, but she did come across a piece about Emily Meeks's memorial in a New Jersey newsletter. Gerry's granddaughter had died of leukemia aged just twenty-three.

The most moving moment of the church service was a speech by her best friend, Georgia Tey, a theater costume designer. To tears and laughter, Georgia revealed that though she and Emily had been friends since they were six, their bond had been cemented as they grew older by a shared love of capybaras and creative poisonings.

"If the FBI had ever gone through the search history of our laptops, we'd have been arrested. Every week, Em and I competed to unlock the puzzle at the heart of whatever mystery we were reading. We'd compare notes over breakfast. If I had a dime for the number of times Emily glanced up from her bagel, knife in hand, and said triumphantly, 'I guessed the murderer before you did!' I'd be a millionaire.

"Emily will live on in every line of every book we ever read together. I'll miss her forever.

Thankfully, I'll always be able rely on Gerry and the rest of the Clue Club to be there in the middle of the night if I call to say, 'I give up . . . How *do* you solve that locked-room murder mystery?'

"I hope you'll join me in three big cheers for Emily and the Clue Club."

"The Clue Club—that's it!" cried Harper. "That's the link between them. All we have to do is work out what the Clue Club is or does."

"I'm a big fan of Sherlock Holmes's old-fashioned methods," Kat conceded, "but when you're racing the clock, sometimes it really does help to have Google."

THIN ICE

"GIVE ME YOUR BEST WILD GUESS, KAT Wolfe," instructed Harper, as if she were a TV quiz mistress. "Don't worry, there are no wrong answers. Is the Clue Club a book club or a robbery club?"

"Maybe both," said Kat, sipping at a tall glass of OJ. She and Harper were both owl-eyed after a much-needed afternoon nap on the sofas with the huskies.

"If that's really how our gangsters met—playing boring board games," Harper went on. "How does the club work? Do they roll the dice remotely, then send Clue challenges by snail mail: 'I suggest it was Colonel Mustard, in the library, with a candlestick... Oh, and by the way, let's steal a priceless painting next Wednesday.' Doesn't seem very practical."

She nudged the box of games she'd rejected with a woolly-socked foot. "Although I have to admit even

I enjoy Clue. Six weapons, six suspects, nine rooms, and three hundred and twenty-four possible solutions. What's not to like?"

"It's easy to like murder mysteries when they're just a game," said Kat, taking another newspaper from the pile she'd brought in from the garage. "*We're* dealing with real humans. There seem to be three hundred and twenty-four possible solutions to our case too, and we can't fathom any of them. Meantime, it's nearly four P.M. The kidnappers could be in Outer Mongolia by now."

"Not unless they've chartered a rocket ship," Harper said drily. "The roads around us are either ice rinks or ski jumps. Anyone driving is risking their lives."

It seemed impossible to believe that the roads would be cleared by the following day, yet their parents insisted they'd be at Nightingale Lodge on Thursday afternoon as planned. The girls had texted them using Harper's home messaging account. Professor Lamb replied in minutes. His flight was on time, and he expected to arrive at the cabin around 4:00 P.M. the next day.

Dr. Wolfe took hours to respond.

Sorry, been at the spa having a facial! So relieved you're coping in the storm. Good news. Lake Placid Car Rental will have a vehicle for me by 2pm tomorrow. I should be with you by 3:30pm.

"A *facial*?" Kat was put out. "I thought she'd be sitting by the phone worrying."

"You told her *not* to worry," Harper reminded her. "Something about being placid in Lake Placid. Do you *want* her to be stressing that we've been buried alive in a blizzard or need our fingers amputated after frostbite?"

Kat was affronted. "I want Mum to be relaxed and happy more than anything on earth. She deserves all the pampering she can handle. It's just that . . . Oh, Harper, I'm so tired, and I miss her and Tiny so much. I love investigating cases with you, and I'm desperate to help Riley, but somehow solving this mystery seems especially hard."

"It does, but like you always say, we know more than we think we do. Breathe. Hug a husky. Or me. It'll turn out okay, I promise."

Humor restored, Kat fetched the scissors. Harper had made lightning progress online. By comparison, Kat's old-fashioned methods had uncovered few useful nuggets. She snipped around the edges of a piece from *USA Today*: DYLAN GUITAR THEFT CAUSES A STINK. The gist of it was that a rare Bob Dylan guitar had vanished from a glass case during a touring exhibition in Austin, Texas. Looking at the timeline, this must have been the gang's first successful robbery.

Shortly before the guitar was snatched, some prankster set off a stink bomb. There'd been a stampede.

No one witnessed the theft. Nobody saw the stink bomb being planted either. A cleaner claimed she glimpsed a "bionic" man sprinting away from the trash area where the smelly device was found. Police didn't believe her.

By now, Harper and Kat had pieced together the basics of every robbery. It was the same story every time. Some kind of distraction followed by a robbery with no witnesses.

"Brenda from the Sleepy-Time Inn was right about the Wish List gang being ghosts," said Kat. "In nine robberies, Riley was the only witness."

Harper looked up from her laptop. "Even ghosts leave traces."

Kat giggled. "What traces do they leave?"

"How should I know? Steam, vapor, smoke . . . Do *you* believe in ghosts, Kat Wolfe?"

"No," Kat said firmly. "I do not. Do you?"

"Not sure," admitted Harper. "I don't believe in ghosts on the internet. Sooner or later everyone leaves footprints online. Not me, naturally, but the average person. The Wish List gang will have left a trail. It's just a question of finding it."

She reached for Kat's watercolor pad. "There's a thread that runs through everything. We're just not seeing it."

WISH LIST CRIMES

1. 1964 Fender Stratocaster Guitar Played by Bob Dylan
2. Green-Enameled Ming "Dragon" Vase
3. 1913 Liberty Head Nickel
4. Lost Eighteenth-Century Masterpiece by Sofia Rossi
5. Rare First Edition of *Where the Wild Things Are* by Maurice Sendak
6. Fifth-Century Bronze Sculpture of a Horse and Hare
7. 1918 Inverted Jenny Stamp
8. Dress Worn by Audrey Hepburn in *My Fair Lady*
9. $50,000,000 Hollinghurst Diamond Necklace

"I've been over and over it," said Kat, "trying to see what links them to the Clue Club, other than a passion for mysteries. Some of the gangsters grew up in the same town, some like nature and wildlife, some have experienced trauma. Rob lost his legs and his career, and Gerry, Bianca, Emilio, and Georgia lost their loved ones to cancer. But there's no one thing that connects all of them. We don't even know for sure if they were all in the Clue Club."

"Let's say we're sort of correct and each of the gang stole one item on the wish list . . . ," said Harper.

"Except for Gerry. We think he stole two."

"Yeah, but he wasn't working alone when he lifted the diamond necklace. Wrong Writer Six told him in the letter: 'Don't be nervous. We've got your back.' WW6 also said there'd be a 'full house' of operatives. The entire gang must have been at the Royal Manhattan that evening. Where's that article you read me on our first night in the cabin?"

Kat dug it out, and they studied it together.

"There were too many dramas during the event for them all to be coincidence," said Kat. "What if we assume that the four climate-change activists who took a blowtorch to the polar bear were Wish List gang members? There was the lobster incident too. A kitchen hand and an accomplice liberated the sad creatures from their tank."

"Good for them." Harper smiled. "Okay, we have six potential members, plus Gerry. Seven. Anyone else? Did we ever find out the name of the shop that caught fire across the street? That was the biggest diversion of the night."

"Fabulous Furs." Kat shivered at the thought of the mink and leopards that had died so that fashion victims could strut about in their coats. "There was something about them in the *New York Post*. But on the night of the fire, the shop was vacant. The owners had gone out of business because they'd been caught selling coats made from endangered animals. Nobody was harmed in the blaze apart from a military veteran. He had to be rescued, suffering from smoke inhalation after his wheelchair got stuck in—"

She stopped and looked at Harper. "You don't think Rob . . . ?"

"If the military vet was a Wish List gangster, our case would break wide open. That's what I think." Harper straightened in her chair, detective radar on red alert. "Kat, what if one reason the Wrong Writers have been so invisible is because the gang members are the kind of people society often doesn't see?"

"You mean, people in wheelchairs, senior citizens, immigrants, climate-change activists, the hired help . . . ?" Were humans really that shallow and insensitive? Kat felt unwell at the thought.

"Precisely," said Harper. "But that doesn't change the fact that the Wish List gangsters are criminal masterminds who may have abducted Riley. Let's not forget about that. Where did you put that article on Bob Dylan's guitar? Didn't the cleaner report seeing a 'bionic' man fleeing the scene after the stink bomb went off?"

"Yep. She called him the 'Blade Runner.'"

Harper looked thoughtful. "Rob uses prosthetics when he's doing his personal training. Says he can run faster than he did when he was playing college football. Other times, he uses his wheelchair, so that would fit too."

Distant thunder rattled the windows. Matty and Rebel raced to the door, whining and growling.

"Each time I think we've seen the back of Storm Mindy, she has a new evil plan to punish us," groaned Harper. "She's dumped a Mount Everest's worth of snow on us, a whole Lake Superior of rain on us, and almost crushed us with a tree branch blown by one of the many gales she's sent our way. Now we have to endure a thunderstorm?"

"For once, Storm Mindy's not to blame," said Kat, peering out of the window. "There's a snowplow clearing the road on the west of the lake."

They both knew what that meant. Once the lane was open, they were on borrowed time.

"Don't panic," said Harper. "It takes a snowplow around seven hours to clear fifteen miles of road, and it's four thirty P.M. now. Even if it continues working overnight, what's the likelihood of the owner turning up before morning?"

Kat didn't reply. She was taking in the utter devastation that they and the huskies had unintentionally wreaked on the cabin. How were they going to fix it before dawn? Apart from anything else, they'd demolished the entire contents of the fridge. The raccoon had helped, but the owner wouldn't believe that.

"Let's take the dogs out and get some air," said Harper. "It'll wake us up, and I need to think."

SILVER LAKE

"IT'S COLDER THAN ANTARCTICA IN THE Adirondacks," said Kat, carving their names in the snow as fog-like steam rose from the icy expanse of Mirror Lake.

"How can it be colder than Antarctica?"

"Thanks to global warming, with no difficulty at all. Didn't you hear about it hitting twenty degrees Celsius on Seymour Island? The penguins were in bikinis. Also, it's summer now in Antarctica; they have the opposite seasons of us. Hey, I've had an idea."

"Ideas would be welcome at this point," Harper said drily.

"First thing tomorrow morning, we put the huskies in the rig, load up our stuff, and take a shortcut across the lake to Nightingale Lodge. We'll drop everything off, race the huskies home to their kennels, and—"

"Cross the lake? No, thanks," Harper interrupted. "We'd go down quicker than the *Titanic*."

"But it's as solid as an ice rink." Kat tossed a pebble and it bounced along the surface. "See?"

Harper picked up a rock and hurled it as far as she could. It hit the ice with a crack and sank without a trace. "Lakes take longer than you'd believe to freeze."

Rebel wanted to chase the rock. He howled in frustration and rushed back and forth along the icy shore.

"The huskies know best," declared Harper. "The ice isn't safe."

She watched the snowplow as it rumbled through the forest to hidden cabins. "Michael Lautner lives on one of the lakes in the Adirondacks," she said thoughtfully. "That magazine story on Rob showed them sitting together on the steps of his cabin. I suppose it's possible that the Lautner brothers and the rest of the gang are hiding out somewhere in the wilderness here."

"You know who else lives on a lake in the Adirondacks," said Kat. "Riley's nan."

"What about her?"

"She's kind, she's a fighter, and she adores Riley. If we could get to her house, we could tell her everything we've learned about the Wish List gang and the Clue Club."

"Everything we've *guessed* about them, you mean."

Kat ignored that part. "Some of what we've found out must be correct. If Riley's nan believes us on the identity of two or three members of the Wish List gang, surely she'll be able to persuade the cops to do the same."

"You could be right," said Harper. "Let's go inside and see if we can find the name of the company that leaked toxic metal into the lake," suggested Harper. "If there was a court case, it'll have been covered by the local press. We might be able to find a phone number for her or an address."

Back in the cabin, Harper did a search. Seconds later, they were looking at a picture of Riley's grandmother, Cath Woodward.

It gave Kat a jolt, seeing her. She was standing in front of a sparkling blue lake on a sunny day. Her hair was purple. Her clothes were largely purple too, swamping her small frame. Her smile reached to the crinkled corners of her eyes.

Kat could imagine Riley's father reading the headline and rolling his eyes. LOON-ATIC! CATH WINS FIGHT TO SAVE SILVER LAKE'S BIRDS.

The girls skimmed through the brief but praise-filled story about Cath's battle to take the owners of a lucrative reptile lamp business to court over toxic dumping. They'd been found guilty. Helpfully, the reporter gave Riley's nan's street address.

Zooming in on Google Earth, Kat and Harper were

able to see the yellow clapboard house in 3D. It was on Silver Lake in the northern Adirondacks, about forty kilometers away from their own cabin on Mirror Lake.

Harper tried for another twenty minutes to find some sort of contact number for Cath Woodward but had to admit defeat. "I'm going to Skype-call the cops. If there's a one-in-a-million chance that we're right about the identity of the gang members, we need to tip them off."

"How are we going to convince them to believe us?" asked Kat. "As soon as they hear a kid on the line, they'll dismiss you as another of those nuts they were complaining about."

"That's why I'm dialing the local county sheriff's office, not nine-one-one. More chance of getting through to a real person— Oh, hi. My name's Harper Lamb. I have some information on the Riley Matthews kidnapping."

There was a loud click and the line buzzed.

Harper rang again. "Before you hang up, this is not a prank, crank, or any other kind of hoax call. We're friends of Riley Matthews, and we believe we know some things that might help you."

"If that's true, you can start by puttin' Mommy or Daddy on the line."

Harper hesitated. "Sir, they're not here right now."

"Little girl, are you aware that wasting police time is a criminal offense?"

"Yes, sir, I am. I'd never do that. If you could hear me out, I'd be so grateful. You might save a girl's life. By a long process of deduction—"

"What now?"

"To cut a long story short, we think we know the identity of some of the members of the Wish List gang. One of them is Michael Lautner, who lives right here in the Adirondacks."

"Miss, you need to give me your name and address."

"Don't forget that there's a million-dollar reward for information leading to Riley Matthews's safe return," Harper said brightly.

There was a long silence.

"Young miss, thanks for calling. I'll be sure to check it out."

ROOKIE ERROR

AT FIRST LIGHT THE NEXT MORNING, KAT slipped a lightweight mesh harness over Nomad's shoulders, adjusted the collar and shoulder pads, and checked the clips.

Though the husky's cut was almost healed and not on the weight-bearing part of her foot, Kat slipped soft red boots over all four of Nomad's paws. She'd done the same with the other five dogs. They'd be traversing unknown terrain. She didn't want to be the cause of any injuries.

Harper watched in fascination from a heap of blankets in a warm corner of the storeroom. "Where did you learn to do that?"

"My mum was the official vet at a British husky-racing demonstration in a London park. I was her unofficial assistant. I watched a lot, learned a little."

Kat smiled as she petted the dogs and untangled a couple of lines. "Don't go mistaking me for someone who has a clue. I've watched a few husky-racing videos, but I've never done this in real life. Never been on a sled and never mushed. There's a high chance we won't make it to the end of the drive."

"Fine by me," said Harper. "If we fail, we fail. At least we'll know we did everything we could to save Riley."

"And vacate the cabin," Kat said with a laugh.

It was 7:02 A.M. on Thursday, the day their parents were due to arrive. A rose dawn outlined the mountain behind Mirror Lake. Storm Mindy had finally moved on, but it had left bitter-cold air behind. Earlier, the girls had raided the prepper cupboard for thermal vests, beanies, gloves, and snow goggles. They'd braved the slippery track to stow their bags in the shed near the kennels. Now they were swaddled in large but ultra-warm clothes. They were as ready as they'd ever be.

To compensate for the food they'd eaten, the broken crockery, and only a feeble attempt at cleaning, Harper had left her vacation pocket money in an envelope on the breakfast bar. She'd decided against adding a note of apology.

"Let them use their imagination about who or what ate their bean chili and slept in their beds. We had to use ours about who they are. They're lucky we're not invoicing them for dog-walking services. There are pet-sitters who'd charge a fortune for taking care of six hyperactive huskies."

"If all we'd done was take care of them, I'd agree," said Kat, who was a semiprofessional pet sitter herself. "The truth is, we dragged their highly valuable pedigree huskies out in a snowstorm on a disastrous expedition to search for our missing friend—"

"They dragged us!"

"Lost them in the snow, and nearly got them mauled by a bear."

"That was my fault," admitted Harper. "I forgot the bear spray."

"We were both to blame," Kat said generously. "We won't make the same mistake twice."

Ironically, it was the conversation with the police officer the previous evening that had galvanized them into taking radical and illegal (they'd be stealing the huskies—at least temporarily) action.

"He's not going to do a thing, is he, Harper?" Kat had fumed after Harper had hung up on Wednesday night.

"I don't believe he is. Or if he does, it'll be because all he cares about is the reward. Infuriating as it is, there's not a whole lot we can do until our parents arrive tomorrow. Once they're here, we'll somehow have to convince them that we might have a chance of saving Riley where detectives have failed."

Kat knew how that conversation would go. Nowhere. She couldn't bear the thought of giving up. Not when they'd worked so hard and made so much progress. If there was one stone left unturned that might lead to Riley's safe return, she and Harper had to find it.

"We have to get to Cath Woodward—Riley's grand-mother. We have to get to Silver Lake."

Harper was incredulous. "Kat, Silver Lake's about twenty-five miles away. How do we get there—call a cab?"

"Husky sled," Kat answered triumphantly.

"*Husky sled?* But you've never driven a husky sled."

"How hard can it be? Huskies are almost as fast as racehorses. I'm not sure how often they need to rest, but if we leave at dawn, we'd get to Riley's nan in two or three hours. With luck and a tailwind."

"And how do we get back?"

"Cath might like us and offer us a lift to Nightingale Lodge?"

"It'd pretty much have to be love at first sight for her to drop everything and drive two strange girls, six huskies, and a sled twenty-five miles through the snow," scoffed Harper. "Plus, she'd need to own an SUV or a horse trailer . . . You're not serious, are you? Have you lost the plot, Kat Wolfe? I'll show you why it's impossible."

She'd spread out the map. "See these contours here? That's a virtual cliff. And that's a marsh packed with whatever crabs, alligators, or northern water snakes live in those things at this time of the year. They'll eat us from the toes up."

"Okay, okay, it's impossible." Kat was deflated.

Harper bent over the map. "Hold on, maybe it's not. Otter Creek runs into Mirror Lake very close to here. There's an excellent chance that it's shallow enough to be frozen solid. If we could drive the huskies to that, we could follow its course to Pinto Pond, which leads to Wild-Goose River, which flows into—"

"Silver Lake!" finished Kat, so excited she could barely breathe. "Harper, do you actually believe it's possible?"

To her great surprise, Harper had. "By using the waterways, we can cut around ten miles off the distance. That'll make it easier on the huskies. But Kat, what happens if we get to Cath Woodward's house and she's the crazy old lady of Wainwright Matthews's nightmares?"

"She won't be," Kat had said confidently. "Riley worships her. According to that article, once Cath was done campaigning to save the loons from the toxic metal monsters, she planned to raise money for a children's hospital. Does that sound crazy to you?"

It was around then that Harper's spirit of adventure had really kicked in. They'd agreed that it was too dangerous to attempt the journey in the dark but planned to leave the next morning at 7:00 A.M., when dawn broke in the wintry Adirondacks. What a thrill it would be to race across the wilderness on a sled pulled by six huskies.

"We need a plan B in case there's no one home when we arrive," Harper had said. "Cath might be away on vacation or off shopping in Manhattan. What do we do then?"

"We face the music," Kat said simply. "If we can get a phone signal, we'll call my mum and explain. If we can't, we'll have to make our way to Nightingale Lodge once the huskies have had a break. Our parents will probably be waiting for us and be beyond furious. We'll be grounded until the end of time. Still, I won't regret it. Everything we're about to do, we're doing to save Riley."

Harper was overjoyed to have made a decision. It felt great to be moving on. They'd had a blast at the Dog House, but cabin fever was setting in. "I'll return the satellite system to the storeroom and put the Raspberry Pi back in its box. Whoever unpacks it will get a shock when they find that it's magically built itself."

"And I'll pack our bags and organize the husky harnesses and lines. Then we should get some sleep."

Before going downstairs, Kat had paused to collect her watercolor pad, Sharpie, and newspaper cuttings. The pad was open at the list of Wish List members.

Gerry Meeks—Retired Insurance Investigator,
   Jersey City, NJ
Emilio D'Angelo—Gardener, Connecticut
Bianca D'Angelo—Artist, Napa Valley, California
Rob Lautner—Personal Trainer, Saratoga, NY
Kiara Thompson—Nurse, Saratoga, NY
Michael Lautner—Lorry Driver, Adirondacks, NY
Georgia Tey, Costume Designer, Jersey City, NJ
Petite woman?

Kat said, "We never did ID the eighth member of the gang. If Georgia's the petite woman, we still have one left to find."

Harper smiled. "We have to leave something for the cops to do, otherwise they'd be redundant."

"Why do you think the gang did it? Greed, or something else?"

"I think that the Clue Club players became so obsessed with trying to solve mysteries that they started to believe they were criminal masterminds themselves. After eight perfect heists, they thought they were invincible."

"They nearly were," said Kat. "If Riley hadn't witnessed the snatching of the diamond necklace, they'd be counting their millions on a yacht somewhere by now. That's why we have to help find her before it's too late. If the Wish List gang can silence her, Gerry Meeks gets a get-out-of-jail-free card."

Harper logged on to the internet one last time. She wanted to wipe the Raspberry Pi's drive before packing it away.

She did a last Google search for Riley Matthews updates. Red headlines popped out at her. Detectives searching for Riley Matthews had finally caught a break. One of the bodyguards had helped a police artist put together a sketch of the man who'd ambushed their vehicle. He'd been dressed in a park ranger's uniform and had shown them a fake badge.

The composite sketch gave Harper the creeps. The man had mean, piggy eyes; two chins; and a hairline that had retreated so far it was making an acquaintance with his neck.

"Hey, Kat. The cops have put out a composite sketch of the man who ambushed the vehicle Riley was traveling in."

"Brilliant, send it to the printer." Kat was on her way down to the storeroom and kept going. "We'll take it to Riley's grandmother in case she hasn't seen it."

Harper didn't answer. She was staring in disbelief at

her screen. A window she thought she'd shut down was still open. Accustomed to her own latest-model, super-secure, firewall-enhanced laptop, it hadn't occurred to her to block the location when she Skype-called the sheriff's office. If the cop she'd spoken to decided to trace the call, he'd be able to pinpoint where the call came from.

It was a rookie error. An inexcusable one.

The only saving grace was that they were in the wrong cabin. Nothing linked them to the Dog House. Provided they left at dawn as planned, there was an excellent chance they'd get away with it. If the police officer who'd taken her call was anything like the state troopers on the TV shows she watched, he'd be stuffing his unshaven face with doughnuts and bad coffee at that hour, boots up on his desk.

Should she tell Kat about her blunder? Harper had concluded that there was no reason to add to Kat's worries. Soon the Dog House would be a distant memory. Everything would be fine.

Now, as the early-morning light filtered through a narrow window, the huskies leaped around the storeroom in a frenzy of anticipation. To them, harnesses meant fun. They meant a thrilling race across the ice or through the snow. They couldn't know how much was at stake.

Harper took a deep breath and allowed herself to put the call to the police officer out of her head. Within minutes, she and Kat and the huskies would be fleeting shadows, further concealed by the banks of Otter Creek.

After that, it wouldn't matter if all the cops in the Adirondacks descended on the Dog House. They might find fingerprints and a bit of a mess, but since the girls didn't have criminal records, that wouldn't help them.

Harper climbed onto the sled with some trepidation.

Kat joined her and gathered up the ganglines, which served as reins.

"Harper, are you *sure* you want to do this? You seem anxious. It's not too late to change your mind. I'll understand, I promise. This could be our most dangerous adventure ever. We're planning to race six huskies across miles of unknown rivers, ponds, and streams that may or may not be frozen. We could fall through the ice, crash, or get attacked by another bear. Or a hostile person. We've got no idea what we'll meet or how Cath Woodward is going to feel about us when we get there. I believe it's worth the risk, but if you don't, just say the word. I'll put the huskies in the kennels, and we'll hike to Nightingale Lodge."

Harper had a sudden memory of her laughing comment to Jet's twins on that first, innocent night in the Adirondacks: *Kat's as brave as a tiger and as loyal as a wolf.*

"Kat, you trust the huskies to keep us safe, don't you?"

Kat adjusted her snow goggles. "They saved us from a charging bear and again in a blizzard. We're their family. I'd trust them—and you—with my life."

"You're my family, and I trust you too," said Harper. "Let's do it."

Kat picked up the storeroom remote control. "It bothers me that we couldn't find Rocky. I've left plenty of food and water for him, but I'd have liked to say goodbye. But we need to get going. As you can tell, as soon as they're in their harnesses, huskies are like thoroughbreds. All they want to do is run."

She was about to open the garage-style door when Nomad barked. Rebel snarled too.

"What's wrong, girl? Rebel, what have you heard?"

A split second later, Kat and Harper heard it too. It was the sound they'd dreaded more than any bear's roar or any thunderstorm.

It was the sinister growl of a car engine.

SAVING RILEY

KAT HUSHED NOMAD, THE LEADER OF THE pack. The other huskies would take their commands from her.

"Harper, if that's the homeowner, we need to get out of here. I'll slip the harnesses off the dogs and press the exit button for the garage door. Hopefully, they'll run around the front of the cabin to greet their musher. We can sneak into the woods at the back."

Harper felt ill. She was certain this disaster was her fault.

"Kat, wait. It might be the cops. They'll have to park at the gate because the driveway's blocked. That'll buy us a couple of minutes. Stay with the huskies and try to keep them quiet. I'll sneak upstairs, see if I can catch a glimpse of the driver. If they're harmless, I'll invent some excuse to get rid of them. If not, I'll scoot back down here. In an emergency, I'll ring the dinner bell twice. If you hear it, let the huskies go and I'll meet you in the woods."

"Harper, I don't think—"

But Harper didn't stop. She was up the storeroom steps in record time. Clambering out, she shut the trapdoor and pulled the rug over it. Tiptoeing to the living room, a worrying thought occurred to her. The cabin door wasn't locked. Harper hoped she'd have time to bolt it from the inside. It was a flimsy lock, but it would be an extra barrier between them and the unwanted visitor.

Keeping out of sight, she peeked through the side window. A police car was parked at the gate. The driver's door was open, making a semicircle of light in the early-morning shadows.

Before Harper could fly back down to the storeroom, boots stamped across the porch. Someone pounded at the door.

Frozen with indecision, she could only watch as the front door handle turned. At the last second, she forced her feet to retreat, but it was too late. A state trooper was stepping into the cabin.

Harper felt a bolt of terror. The officer matched the composite sketch of the man responsible for ambushing Riley's bodyguards' vehicle. He'd shaved since and changed his uniform from park ranger to cop, but otherwise it was a remarkable likeness, right down to his mean, calculating expression.

A zen stillness came over Harper. A tip Kat had mentioned from the Adirondacks survival book returned to her with perfect clarity.

Your brain is your biggest asset . . . Those people that remain calm, don't panic, and then logically reason out their situation are the ones who most often survive.

"Good morning!" she chirped in the manner of a waitress welcoming a favored customer to a diner. "I was just on my way to answer the door." She eyed the badge on his chest: OFFICER BURT SKINNER.

The officer's brow jutted over his pebble eyes like an eroded cliff. "Who are you? Where's the musher?"

"He's out exercising the huskies," improvised Harper. "You've just missed him. He'll be gone for hours. Would you like me to pass on a message?"

"Isn't that interesting." Officer Skinner began to roam around the room, taking in the scattered foam cushion innards, the dishes piled in the sink, the ash spilling from the grate. "And you'd be what—his daughter?"

"Uh-huh. Like I said, he'll be gone for a while. Maybe you could come back later."

"I could, but then again I might make myself a coffee first. That okay with you, young miss?"

He strolled into the kitchen and filled the coffeepot with water. "What did you say your name was?"

Harper hovered by the breakfast bar, torn between convincing him to leave and making a break for the storeroom. Her mind raced. Why would a police officer dressed as a park ranger attack Riley's bodyguards? Was he a cop at all or just pretending?

But, no, he had to be the real deal. It was him who'd taken her call at the sheriff's office, she was certain of it. The "young miss" was a giveaway. Was it possible that there was an extra member of the Wish List gang she and Kat hadn't counted on? A crooked cop would make a perfect robber. Maybe he'd planned to eliminate the star witness so the trial would collapse, freeing his accomplice, Gerry Meeks.

Whatever the truth, he was a cunning and deadly monster who had already put two trained protection officers in the hospital. It was unbelievable bad luck that of all the cops in all the sheriff's departments in the U.S., Harper had gotten him on the end of the line. Now he believed that someone in the Dog House had information on Riley's whereabouts.

"Umm, uh, my name's Louise," she told him. "There's a to-go cup in the cupboard behind you. Take it with you! Drop it off next time you're passing. You're welcome to have the bag of Reese's Peanut Butter Cups too."

He propped himself against the counter, head cocked to one side. "Maybe I will. Maybe I won't. 'Fore I do anything, though, Louise, you and I need to have words. See, Torvill, the Norwegian widow who owns the huskies, she only ever hires women mushers to take care of 'em. Says they're more reliable. Not sayin' I agree with that, but they're her huskies. It's her choice. The clue's in the team name: Wonder Women Racing.

"Other thing is, Torvill's a real stickler for tidiness. Any time I been around here, you could eat off the floor. But right now it's like a grenade went off in a cushion factory."

Out of the corner of her eye, Harper noticed a cereal box wobble. Rocky's masked-bandit features rose above the box of granola before sinking out of sight. If she hadn't been so scared, she'd have laughed. She did her best to focus on the sallow jowls of Officer Skinner—if that was his real name—while edging carefully around the counter.

He blocked her path. "You seem pretty bundled up, Louise, for a kid who claims to only be hanging around the cabin, not bothering to wash the dishes. Sure you're not off to the North Pole like one of them explorers?"

"I was going to out with Dad and the huskies, but I changed my mind."

He snorted. "Call me suspicious, Louise, but what I'd like to know is why you've been lying to me since

I arrived. You're averaging about one lie per minute. First, you lied about what you and your dad are doing in Torvill's cabin—"

"We're visiting!"

"If that was true, you'd be at the Royal Victoria Hospital in Montreal, Canada. That's where she was taken for an emergency operation after suffering a burst appendix on an overnight dog-training trip. There were complications, and she was sedated for a few days. When she came around last night, she was frantic about her huskies—understandably. Asked us to check up on them."

Harper nearly fainted. That explained why the huskies had been left alone. She and Kat were going to be arrested, exactly as they'd feared.

But the cop hadn't finished.

"Next, you told a lie about the huskies going out in the snow 'for hours.' I ain't deaf. They're whining and scuffling fit to blow a gasket down in the basement. And I'll take a punt that Louise is not your real name. That's lie number three. Fourth, you're lying about why you're dressed for a polar expedition. Fifth, you made up lies about Riley Matthews's kidnappers. Yeah, I know it was you on the phone, *Louise*. I traced your call to this here cabin."

He lunged at her and clutched her arm. "Start talking, kid, or you'll be walking all the way to the jailhouse."

"Ow, you're hurting me."

He squeezed even harder. "Where is that Riley brat?" he thundered. "I had a tip-off that she knows where the diamond necklace is stashed. Where is she hiding? *Urff!!!*"

He dropped Harper's arm and reeled away, blood streaming from two punctures on his neck. Chittering in terror, the raccoon jumped from his shoulder onto the kitchen cabinet. The husky cookie jar smashed as he evaded the man's grasp and leaped for his escape route.

Before disappearing, the raccoon pivoted toward Harper as if to reassure himself that she didn't need his help anymore.

"Go, Rocky!" she screamed.

Officer Skinner was clawing at a roll of paper towels. The raccoon was forgotten as he clamped a wad to his bleeding neck.

Harper didn't waste time concerning herself with his well-being. She ran for the front door. Slamming it behind her, she jumped off the porch into the snow.

All she could think about was leading him away from Kat. Once she'd done that, she'd try to flee into the woods.

The man staggered out onto the porch after her. "Come back here or you're dead."

Harper kept going, sloshing and crunching through the snow on the driveway, her breath coming in gasps.

When she reached the police car, she leaned into the driver's side, wrinkling her nose at the stench of stale sweat, festering burger wrappers, and crumpled coffee cups. Burt Skinner was hardly in a position to give lectures on cleanliness.

Wrenching the keys from the ignition, she rushed down to the lakeshore and threw them as hard and far as she could. They slid into a crack in the ice and were lost to view.

Officer Skinner was standing on a rise glaring down at her. "You've done it now, Louise. You and Riley Matthews, you'll be sorry."

As soon as Rocky came shooting down the storeroom pipe, gibbering with fear, Kat knew that Harper was in desperate trouble.

At the time, she was standing beside the printer. While poking around the prepper cupboard for dog treats to keep the huskies quiet, she'd spotted the police sketch Harper had uploaded for her. The fake park warden who'd ambushed the vehicle Riley was traveling in looked every inch a bully with a badge. She could imagine him arresting people just because he could.

While at the printer, Kat noticed something else too. Harper had reprinted the photos from the Royal Manhattan in hope of improving the detail. She'd forgotten to pack them. As Kat slid them into her backpack, she spotted what looked to be the white flare of a flashbulb on one of the pictures.

But there wasn't a moment to think about it as Rocky came flying out of the pipe and leaped into Kat's arms. That was too much for the agitated huskies. They barked and howled loudly enough to be heard in Florida.

Remembering Harper's instructions on what to do in an emergency, Kat made a series of spontaneous decisions.

She stuffed Rocky into her backpack, zipped up his protests, and heaved him onto her shoulders. Leaping onto the sled, she snatched the ganglines and popped open the garage doors. As cold air blasted in, the huskies blasted out.

"Gee!" cried Kat. "Gee, gee!"

The huskies swerved left. As they rounded the front of the cabin, Kat got the shock of her life. In the distance, Harper was stumbling along the lakeshore. A barrel-shaped police officer lumbered after her, a bloodied scarf of paper towels billowing from his neck.

With a collective howl of rage, the huskies bore down on him.

"Leave it! On by!" Kat screamed as they drew level with the cop.

Five of the huskies obeyed—albeit with great reluctance—but Thunder swung his head as they swept past, delivering a vicious nip.

The man skidded on the ice and went down like a felled buffalo. He lay on his ample belly, yelling curses.

Kat braked long enough to pull Harper onto the rig, hugging her close with one arm and clinging to the lines with the other. They bounced and wobbled along the lake's edge toward Otter Creek.

Kat's heart was in her mouth. Would the ice be solid enough to take their combined weight? The huskies would know. She had to trust them.

They did, and it was.

The minute they were sheltered by the high, rocky walls of the creek, the tortured yells of the police officer faded to nothing. The huskies quickly found their stride. They ran in silence, their breath blowing in white puffs, their bright blue eyes watching for hazards.

Snow-covered evergreen trees hung like specters over the banks. Though the wind numbed their cheeks and sliced through Kat's thermal gloves, the fire in her chest blazed strongly.

"Who was that man, Harper? Did he hurt you?"

Harper recounted her conversation with the officer and her terror when she'd realized he matched the sketch of the ambush attacker. It had changed everything.

Theirs was no longer a mission only to save Riley. She and Harper had to get to safety *now*!

Rocky too, Kat remembered with a smile, as the raccoon poked his head out of the backpack.

One after the other, landmarks the girls had circled on the map and rehearsed until they were dizzy fell behind them. Deadwood Bridge. Pinto Pond. Wild-Goose River.

Before they knew it, the huskies were puffing up the riverbank. Silver Lake, iced over and streaked the color of mercury, was before them.

Harper saw the pale-yellow house first. Smoke wafted from the chimney. "Kat, that's Cath Woodward's home at the end of the lane. I recognize it from the satellite image. Seems we're in luck. I think she's home."

"Haw," Kat called to the dogs. "Haw!"

Panting noisily, the huskies veered right and pulled up behind a battered SUV. A sign planted in the snow-covered lawn appealed to visitors to: SAVE ST. FRANCIS OF ASSISI CHILDREN'S HOSPITAL.

"Hold on to the huskies," said Harper. "I'll ring the doorbell." She walked confidently up the path of the clapboard house.

Kat stared at the hospital sign, remembering the local newspaper report: "With the battle to save the loons behind her, Woodward plans to turn her attention to fundraising for the St. Francis of Assisi Children's Hospital . . ."

Riley's words also came back to her: *My nan's crazy about birds. Dad thinks she's crazy in every way, but that's only because she's as fierce as a lioness when it comes to righting wrongs.*

Righting Wrongs.

Wrong Righters.

Wrong Writers.

"Harper, stop!"

Abandoning the huskies, Kat ran up the path.

It was too late.

Petite, purple-haired Cath Woodward was opening the door, her smile turning to astonishment as she took in the six huskies spreading out across her lawn, the bedraggled girls in their oversized thermals, and Rocky the raccoon, shrieking to be let out of Kat's rucksack.

Kat bounded onto the porch. To Harper's astonishment, she said furiously, "It's you, isn't it? You're the eighth member of the Wish List gang or the Wrong Writers or Clue Club or whatever stupid name you call yourselves. How could you do it? You've betrayed your own granddaughter, made her a pawn in your evil game. She loves you so much. Are you going to claim the reward for kidnapping her too?"

A tall man with many tattoos and a gentle gaze came up behind Riley's grandmother. "Is there a problem, Cath?"

"Hope not," she said. "Any chance you could feed and water these girls' huskies, Michael? They look as if they might need it."

His face lit up. "It would be a pleasure."

"Don't you dare touch them!" Kat began angrily, but Harper quieted her with a *We have more pressing business* glance.

Cath Woodward looked sad and resigned, as if the fight had gone out of her.

"I don't believe you'd abduct your own grand-daughter," said Harper. "So what have you done with her? Where's Riley?"

"I think you'd better come in."

Kat tried to resist, but Harper was already unlacing her snowy boots and following Cath into the house, and she wasn't sure what else to do. Whispering soothingly to the raccoon, she stepped over the threshold.

The hallway was lit with candles and smelled of warming winter spices.

Classical music played softly. Cath hung up their coats and gloves before leading them up a staircase lined with photos of sailboats and birds. Kat noticed a portrait of a flame-haired woman who resembled Riley.

Cath pushed open a bedroom door and Kat's mouth dropped open. Riley was sitting up in bed, wearing candy-striped pajamas. She was absorbed in the game of

Scrabble she was playing with Bianca and Georgia. Kat recognized the women from their online photos. Bianca gave a nervous smile. Georgia threw a questioning glance at Cath and an alarmed one at Rocky.

"Riley," said Cath. "Two friends are here to see you. Three, if you count the raccoon."

"I keep telling you, I don't have any friends," said Riley, intent on rearranging the letters she concealed behind a fold of patchwork quilt. "Except y'all, of course . . . Uh, what raccoon?"

When she saw Kat, her expression flickered through more moods than Storm Mindy. It settled on partly sunny with a warning of thundershowers to come.

"Kat with a *K*! Harper! What are you doing here? How did you find me?"

"They know everything," Cath Woodward said in a flat tone. "Don't ask me how. They know about the Wish List gang, the Clue Club . . . even the Wrong Writers."

"No!" cried Bianca.

"Are the cops here?" asked Georgia.

Riley's eyes met Kat's. There was an audible gulp.

"This is not how it looks," she said.

WHAT THREE WORDS

"BEFORE YOU GET MAD AND REFUSE TO speak to me ever again, I want to thank you for saving my life, Kat with a *K*."

With those words, Riley scrambled out of bed, had a head rush, and collapsed weakly onto the patchwork quilt. Bianca went to put a protective arm around her, but Riley twisted away. She rearranged the pillows and sat cross-legged on the bedcovers.

Kat was simmering with fury. "Saving *your* life? We risked our own lives and the lives of the huskies to go searching for you in a snowstorm. We were nearly killed by a bear. And the entire time you were fine and cozy in Silver Lake, playing Scrabble with your nan and other criminals."

"We deserve that," remarked Georgia.

"Hard to argue with the 'other criminals' part," agreed Bianca.

"That's one story, but it's not the *whole* story," said Riley. "If you know everything, Kat, then you'll know that when I met you in the forest, I wasn't with my aunt and uncle. They were protection officers, hired after I witnessed the theft of a diamond necklace. It was their job to keep me safe until the trial."

"How did they feel about your grandmother being a dear friend of the accused?" demanded Kat. "Or did it slip your mind to mention it? Were you in on the scam too? Were you planning to have an attack of amnesia at the trial?"

"Whoa there!" protested Georgia. "Be upset with us, sure, but leave Riley out of it. She's innocent."

Cath Woodward laid a hand on her granddaughter's shoulder. "Believe us, or don't. Until yesterday, Riley knew nothing of the Clue Club. The fact that she saw Gerry take the diamond necklace at the Royal Manhattan was a cruel coincidence, and finding out that her grandmother was involved was crueler still—for both of us. When her bodyguards were ambushed and the identity of the star witness was revealed, I died a thousand deaths."

"If you really didn't know that your nan was a gangster and a thief, you must have felt betrayed," said Harper.

"That's if Riley's telling the truth," interjected Kat.

"Stick around long enough and I'll prove it," Riley shot back. "Yeah, I felt lied to and let down. Nan used to be my hero."

Her grandmother looked as if she wanted to crawl under the bed, but Riley had already moved on. She stared at the girls in wonder. "Why would you put your life on the line for someone you've met only once, Kat? Harper, you didn't know me at all. Why would either of you risk so much for me? After today, I'd understand if you withdrew your offer of friendship, but I'll always be a friend to both of you—if you need an extra one. When someone saves your life, that's just the way it is."

Harper was bewildered. "You keep saying that, but I don't understand. How did we save you?"

"I'll try to explain. Technically, it was Kat's cat who saved me."

Kat felt a rush of joy. "Tiny helped you?"

"No question about it. Without the photo you gifted me, I wouldn't be here."

"Tell us what happened," urged Harper. "Leave nothing out."

"I hate to be boring," Georgia broke in, "but do either of you girls have a phone signal? I need to message Riley's dad. He'll be out of his mind with worry."

Harper checked hers. "Nope, we might as well be on the moon."

Kat was looking from Riley to her grandmother and back again. "Mr. Matthews doesn't know that Riley's been rescued?"

"He's known since yesterday morning that she's safe, but we haven't plucked up the courage to give him Cath's address yet," confessed Georgia. "He's changed his phone number, and Riley doesn't have the new one. We had no choice but to call the police hotline. For nearly a day, they wouldn't believe us. Then they wanted an address. I was on the phone to them and I hung up in a panic. Before we could decide what to do next, the power got knocked out. That was last night. Michael was on his way to the gas station to use their phone to call the hotline again when you and your huskies showed up."

Riley put an arm around her grandmother. "It's a complicated situation. After my mom walked out two years ago—"

"Walked out? I was wondering if she'd died," Harper admitted.

"Nah, she just moved to New Zealand with her personal trainer and started a new family. To cope, Dad threw himself into work. That's all he does these days: work, work, work. It's been tough. Nan and I were always super close—much closer than me and my mom were. She had no interest in reading and couldn't stand the outdoors, but that didn't matter because me and

Nan were bonded by nature and books. But after Mom left, Dad banned me from seeing my grandmother. He said she was a bad influence."

"Gee, I can't imagine why," Harper said sarcastically.

Riley flushed. "Obviously, he didn't know she was a *robber*."

Cath Woodward put her head in her hands. "How on earth did it come to this?"

"Dad was more concerned that she'd turn me into an eco-warrior like her," explained Riley. "He doesn't understand that even though I was born smack-bang in the middle of Manhattan, the wilderness is in my blood. That's why your wild cat helped me so much, Kat. After the ambush, what kept me going in the storm was this absolute belief that Tiny and the forest animals—and you and Harper, of course—were my friends."

"But how did you get from there to here?" said Harper. "To this house?

"I'll tell you the bits I remember. Nan can fill in the rest. At about four A.M. on Tuesday, I was woken by the burglar alarm on our safe house. Jo was sure it was a bear, but she and Tony made the decision to move me to another cabin just in case. They rushed me to the vehicle in my pj's and a denim jacket.

"I dozed off in the back seat. Next thing I was shocked awake by gunshots. We were parked, and the driver's door was open. Tony was lying bleeding on the road. I couldn't see the shooter. Jo pulled me out of the vehicle and got me into the trees by the roadside. She gave me her phone and told me to run and hide. She promised to come get me. About five minutes later, I heard another shot, and then there was just a horrible silence. After that, I just ran and ran."

"You must have been terrified," said Harper, recalling the police brute who'd crushed her arm just a few hours ago, demanding to know where Riley was hidden. Now didn't seem the right moment to mention it.

"Mainly, I was terrified of getting hypothermia," Riley was saying. "Like I told Kat, up until two years ago, I came to these woods all the time. Winter or summer, Nan would take me camping. She taught me survival techniques. I knew I had to dig a snow cave to keep warm. I didn't manage that, but I did build a shelter."

"We found it," Kat told her.

"*You did?*" Riley was amazed.

"Matty, one of our huskies, tracked you there using the blue neckerchief you gave me."

"If only I'd had her fur to heat me up in the storm. My pajamas and sneakers were soaked and crusty with snow. I couldn't feel my feet or my hands. All I wanted to do was sleep. But I knew from what Nan had taught me that that's the biggest danger sign. It means that hypothermia's setting in."

"What about the bodyguard's phone?" asked Kat. "Did you try using it?"

"A thousand times. There was no signal, and the battery was dying. Eventually, I got so cold I didn't care about living anymore. I started to drift off. Suddenly, I heard your voice, Kat, as clear as if you'd been standing beside me. 'He looks scary, but he's the best friend anyone could ever have. He's my protector, and I'm sure he wouldn't mind being yours.'

"I remembered you passing me the photo. Your hands were so warm and your eyes were so kind. You'd told me you'd be my friend. I took the photo from the pocket of my denim jacket. Tiny did look scary but in a good way, like he'd protect me from any bear, assassin, or storm. His leopard fur was so silky and golden, it made me feel better just to look at it. I wanted to stay alive just so if I ever saw you again I could tell you that Tiny's spirit saved me in the snow. I didn't know then . . ."

Her voice trailed away.

Her grandmother read her thoughts. "You couldn't have guessed that when your paths crossed again it would be under these unfortunate circumstances. I'm so sorry, Riley. If I could go back in time and change things, I would."

Bianca and Georgia shuffled awkwardly too.

"You still haven't answered Harper's question, Riley," said Kat. "How did you get from there to here?"

Riley rallied. "While I was shining the phone flashlight on the photo of Tiny, I noticed the signal flickering. I saw something else too: Jo had installed What3Words on her phone."

"What's that?" asked Kat.

"An app that divides the earth into three-meter squares and gives each square a three-word locator," said Harper.

Riley smiled. "Nan had made me put it on my own phone in case we ever got separated on a camping trip. My brain was so cold and fuzzy, I couldn't recall Dad's new number, but Nan's was engraved on my brain. My fingers were too numb to send a message. I just prodded the locator and hoped she'd figure out it was me. That's the last thing I remember until I woke up here—in this den of thieves."

Cath sagged as if she'd been dealt a physical blow. "By a grim stroke of fortune, it was only because I was up at dawn checking the headlines to see if the cops were getting anywhere in their hunt for us—the so-called Wish List gang—that I saw the breaking news. It was the single most hideous moment of my life, discovering that the star witness was none other than my own grand-daughter. Worse, Riley was missing, feared abducted or lost in the northern Adirondacks with Storm Mindy charging in.

"There are no words to describe how I felt. It was

my fault she was in that situation. If we'd never come up with that wretched Wish List, she wouldn't be in harm's way."

"What did you do next?" asked Kat.

"As I despaired, my phone pinged with a notification from What3Words. Three words came up: *Sweetcorn. Hare. Volcano.* The number wasn't Riley's, but there was no doubt in my mind that it must be her. I rang Michael, who's taking care of your huskies, and he and I drove like maniacs in our truck to the red square that marked Riley's grid reference on my phone. The whole way there, it pulsed like a beating heart.

"When we found her, she was virtually lifeless. With the storm moving in, it wasn't safe or practical to get her to a hospital. Our friend Kiara's a nurse and could give her the best care. She and her husband, Rob, had been staying with Michael, so it was simple enough to transfer their bags here. Our other friends were already on their way to join us. When Storm Mindy arrived, the seven of us—and Riley—were trapped here."

"I finally came around yesterday morning," said Riley. "You can imagine how I felt when Nan broke the news that she and the others were the subject of an international manhunt and close friends with the thief I'd watched snatch the diamond necklace."

"What made it even worse," said Bianca, "is that it's because of us—the Clue Club—that Riley's bodyguards were ambushed. After Gerry was arrested, we were so desperate to get him out of jail that we were clutching at straws. Gerry used the one phone call he was allowed to tell my dad, Emilio, that he didn't have the necklace. We believed him. Dad called the cops anonymously and asked them to investigate whether the star witness was actually the thief. We had no idea that Riley was the star witness or that some maniac would take those words as truth and attack the bodyguards. I guess he wanted to steal the diamond necklace for himself."

Bianca looked stricken. "Now we're in quite a tangle. A pickle, as you Brits would say."

"Yes, we are," mumbled Cath Woodward. "As soon as we get a phone signal, I'm going to call the cops and tell them that Riley is here with me. I suspect that Riley's dad will be here within hours. We're not sure how much or how little to tell him."

"We also need to get Gerry out of jail," fretted Bianca, "but we can't do that without confessing to being in the Wish List gang. It's a calamity."

"How did it start?" asked Kat. "You just don't seem the type to steal fifty million dollars' worth of diamonds."

"That's a whole other story," said Georgia.

Cath put up her hand. "One that might best be enjoyed with cake and company. Shall we go downstairs and join the others?"

ONE GOOD TURN

AFTER DAYS OF FENDING FOR THEMSELVES, it was lovely to be taken care of. Kat felt guilty that she didn't feel more guilty about hanging out with criminals. It seemed the most natural thing in the world to be crammed into Cath's living room with seven crooks, six dozing huskies, Harper, Riley, and the raccoon, who was curled up in Georgia's arms as if he belonged there.

"This is what we serve at every Clue Club meeting," said Cath, dishing out raspberry and coconut slices and the remains of an orange polenta cake. "There's coffee for those who want it, and we always have homemade lemonade or ginger beer—like the Famous Five."

A thrill went through Kat. They were honorary members of the mysterious Clue Club.

Then she remembered that Cath wasn't a sweet old grandmother, any more than Gerry Meeks was a sweet old granddad. If even half of what she and Harper had deduced was accurate, these were professional thieves with a multi-million-dollar haul of art and jewels to show for it. Kat scanned the room for any sign of the swag. Was the diamond necklace hidden in plain sight in Cath's apparently humble house?

"Where do we begin?" Kiara asked anxiously.

"We begin at the beginning, with Gerry, half a century ago," said her husband.

"Half a century?" gasped Harper.

Rob laughed and rolled his wheelchair nearer the fire. "Forty-eight years, to be precise. We have to begin with Gerry, because without him there'd be no Clue Club and without the Clue Club, there'd be no us."

Some strong emotion rippled through the room. Kat realized that whatever else they'd done, the friends cared deeply for one another.

Emilio, a handsome Italian, set aside his coffee cup. "Like so many things, the Clue Club started with the best of intentions. Gerry was a brilliant insurance investigator, but his job was immensely stressful and he traveled nonstop. Perhaps inevitably, his marriage broke up. His wife remarried and moved away, taking his daughter with her.

"Throughout that difficult time, books were Gerry's constant companions. Sources of comfort and bringers of laughter, hope, kindness, and adventure. Most of all, he loved mysteries."

"Like me and Harper," said Kat.

"And me," said Riley.

"Join the club!" said Bianca, and everyone laughed.

Georgia took up the story. "Gerry's daughter grew up and became a high-flying New York City executive. She regularly called on him to babysit his grand-daughter, Emily. He had more time on his hands then, and he'd spend hours reading to her. As Emily got older, she caught his passion for mysteries. At school, Emily and I became best friends. Pretty soon, I was hooked on mysteries too. We formed our own Clue Club. Emily wrote us a funny mission statement. She said it would be a book club for readers who like 'living dangerously.' That's how she put it."

Bianca laughed. "We still have her mission statement. She said that in order to join, members had to relish cliff-hangers, twists, red herrings, and heart-racing suspense. Most important, readers had to vow to fight every day for justice, mercy, and the truth."

Kat wanted to burst out, *What would any of you know about justice and truth?* But she had a feeling there was more to the story.

"It wasn't until Gerry moved to Shady Oaks three years ago—against Emily's wishes—that the Clue Club became a permanent part of our lives," Bianca went on. "Papa had been hired to take care of the gardens. He, Gerry, and I discovered a shared love of mysteries. In time, I introduced Rob, Kiara, and Michael to our little book club."

"After Emily died, Gerry became one of my closest friends," said her father, Emilio. "I'd lost my own daughter to cancer, so I knew how he felt. I was forced out of Shady Oaks, but we wrote letters every week. That's what makes this situation so unbearable. While we're sitting here, eating cake, Gerry's in a windowless cell. Because of us. Because of the Clue Club."

"We'll make this right," Cath said grimly. "I don't know how, but we will."

"I suppose it was around the time Rob had his accident that we realized that the Clue Club had become more than a book club," said Georgia. "It was a life club. We'd become family. We were there for one another through thick and thin. We nicknamed ourselves the Wrong Writers—a play on words. We righted wrongs. If any of us had a cause—a fundraising raffle for the local animal shelter, or a campaign to save loons—the others would help."

"That's how I got involved," Cath told Riley. "Michael lives in the Adirondacks too, and he introduced me to the Clue Club. When we weren't swapping clues on our latest mystery, we were fighting for the loons or trying to raise money for St. Francis of Assisi Children's Hospital."

"How did it go from being a life club to a criminal club?" Kat asked bluntly. "At what stage did you stop righting wrongs and start doing wrong?"

"Let me guess," said Harper. "You decided to use the sleuthing skills you'd learned from novels to get away with stealing every luxury you'd ever dreamed of?"

"No!" cried Bianca.

"Not exactly," said Rob.

"It wasn't like that," insisted Cath Woodward. "Not at first."

"What was it like?" demanded Riley.

"It all started two years ago when Gerry saw a magazine photo of Cynthia Hollinghurst wearing her diamond necklace," said Rob. "He was livid about it. It was only then that he admitted to being haunted by the only insurance case he ever lost."

Kat leaned forward. "What was it?"

"He called it the 'Case of the Missing Blood Diamonds.' You'll have heard of conflict diamonds, I expect. Diamonds mined using child and other slave labor in conditions of unimaginable hardship and wickedness. Clancy Hollinghurst, Cynthia's father, is rumored to have made his fortune from such a mine in the Democratic Republic of Congo in Africa.

"Thirty years ago, Clancy claimed thirty million

dollars from Gerry's insurance company after an apparent break-in at his home. The cops never caught the intruder. Gerry was convinced that the robbery was invented, and Clancy knew he knew the truth. Yet he was so arrogant and certain he'd never be found out, he used to taunt Gerry about it. Gerry did everything he could to prove the man a liar and a fraudster but never managed it. Clancy got away with both the diamonds and a thirty-million-dollar insurance payout."

"Fast-forward a couple of decades," said Bianca, "and there is Clancy's daughter Cynthia brazenly wearing the very diamonds that were supposedly stolen but designed to look completely different. Gerry showed us the magazine profile on her. The gems were now worth an incredible fifty million dollars."

"At the time," Cath explained, "we were trying to raise that exact amount of money to build a hospital unit for children with cancer in the Adirondacks, a place where they could heal and be with nature. After months of fund-raising, we had a measly ten grand. It seemed hopeless."

"I can imagine the conversation," said Harper. "Somebody joked that if you stole one, you could pay for the other."

"Gerry only said what each of us was thinking," Bianca told her. "If we took the blood diamonds that had been mined by suffering children and exploited by a fraudster, and found a way to sell them—maybe as individual diamonds—we could use the money to ease the suffering of children with cancer, maybe some small good would come out of those sad jewels."

"Since Gerry's in jail and the diamonds are missing, I suppose it wasn't quite so simple," said Kat.

"No," muttered Cath. "It was not."

"We prided ourselves on our cleverness," said Emilio. "We were sure we'd get away with stealing the necklace. We didn't realize we were building our own gilded cage."

"If anyone's to blame for how things have turned out, it's me," said Rob. "I came up with the stupid wish list. At first, it was all just a game, like Clue. I kidded that since we weren't proper thieves, we'd each have to practice snatching something. We wrote out a funny robbers' wish list. A Ming vase, a priceless painting, and so on. It's not so funny now."

"What did you steal first?" asked Harper, intrigued.

"The next weekend, Rob and I went to a musical instrument exhibition in Austin, Texas," Michael said. "Rob noticed a guitar that Bob Dylan had supposedly played, only nobody knew for sure. It was worth a million dollars. We couldn't believe it. Rob tried asking the merchant about it, but the man turned ugly and said that Rob's wheelchair was putting off customers and costing him business."

"I was furious, but Rob said that the man's attitude would make stealing the guitar a walk in the park. He bet me that if he returned the next day in his prosthetics, set off a stink bomb, and walked off with the guitar, no one would remember him. He was right. It was easy. We'd stolen the guitar and gotten away with it. We were thieves."

"We were thieves with a code of honor," Cath reminded him. "We had rules. The necklace aside, we couldn't take anything that was worth more than a thousand dollars—in our opinion, that is—and every item had to be carefully stored within a one-mile radius of the theft, so it could be returned a week later."

"If everything you stole has been returned, why are the cops still hunting for you?" demanded Harper.

"That plan went awry early on," admitted Michael. "We were victims of our own success. We decided to wait for things to cool off, but each time we got away with a new heist, our notoriety grew. The press started calling us the Wish List gang."

"How can you say that you never stole anything worth more than one thousand dollars?" accused Harper. "You took a Liberty nickel worth nearly four million."

"Oh, please," said Michael. "It's a five-cent coin. How can it be worth four million? Who decides these things? Anyhow, it's quite safe and will be returned just as soon as we can be sure we won't go to jail for giving it back."

"What about the priceless painting you snatched?" Kat said, looking at Bianca.

Bianca laughed. "Sofia Rossi, the artist, was one of my ancestors. She was a good but eccentric nun and an amateur artist. Papa and I used to laugh about a note she'd written on the back of a ghastly painting of a poppy field. She'd called it *The Lost Masterpiece of Sofia Rossi*. As an experiment, we sent it to a modern art gallery in New Orleans. They loved it but wouldn't pay us for it. Then, when I stole it back, they claimed it was worth over one million dollars."

"None of us are laughing now," Cath reminded them sternly. "Because of the Clue Club, Gerry's in jail, Riley nearly died in the storm, and these girls nearly got themselves killed looking for her. I wish I could wave a magic wand and put things back to how they were, but I wouldn't know where to start."

"Why don't you do what you intended to do in the beginning?" suggested Kat. "Return all the stolen items to the art galleries or wherever."

"It's tricky when there's a nationwide manhunt for us," said Michael.

"Send an anonymous email to the cops," Harper told him. "Tell them where you've stashed the goods. I'll show you how to do it without being traced."

"But that doesn't help Gerry," said Emilio. "We

might save our own skins, but unless we can find the necklace, he'll still be rotting in jail. I can't live with that."

"I can get him out," announced Riley. "I'll—what's the word?—take back my testimony."

"Recant," supplied her grandmother.

"I'll recant my testimony. Say that I made it all up to get attention. Dad and the cops will be angry with me, but it'll be worth it. Gerry will be free. Without my witness statement, the case will collapse."

"No," said her grandmother. "Gerry knew the risk he was taking. We all did. When you're on the witness stand, you'll be under oath. You'll swear to tell the truth and nothing but the truth."

"But, Nan—"

"No buts. Two wrongs don't make a right."

"Is there any way you could have been mistaken, Riley?" asked Harper.

"I know what I saw, and so did Gerry," Riley said stubbornly. "When he glanced up and realized I'd seen him put the diamond necklace in his pocket, his face was sick with shame and guilt."

Kat asked, "What happened immediately after that?"

"Cynthia screamed when she realized her diamonds were gone. There was a stampede in the ballroom. There were celebrities having panic attacks thinking the hotel was on fire, and politicians being raced out by their bodyguards. The Force Ten security guards came tearing in, smelling of smoke and trying to work out what was going on."

"Where was Gerry?"

"He disappeared in the chaos. I thought he'd escaped. I told Dad I'd witnessed the theft. He shouted for the guards, and they found Gerry sitting on the corner of a fake iceberg, looking like his world had just ended. My heart kind of broke for him, but as far as I was concerned, he didn't have to steal the necklace. He could have chosen not to be a thief. If I'd known he was stealing it to help build a hospital for sick children, I might have done things differently."

"If you don't like the way the story ends, maybe it's not the end of the story," said Kat.

"What do you mean?" Emilio asked sharply.

Kat took the hotel photos from her backpack. "We printed these off the Royal Manhattan website. In this picture, it's obvious from Riley's expression that she's seen Gerry take the necklace. In this one, taken minutes later, Gerry's visible from behind. There's a trolley going by on one side of him, and a waiter with a tray of smoked salmon on ice on the other. The waiter's bewildered, and there are people running in the background, like Riley described. But look at the streak of silver on the left of the photo."

She passed the picture around the room. "At first,

I thought it was a flash from the camera, but when I studied it more closely, I realized it was something else entirely. What do you see?"

Riley gasped. "The diamond necklace. Gerry must have felt guilty about taking it, tried to fish it out of his pocket, and then dropped it."

At that instant, Kat caught sight of the clock. "It's nearly lunchtime! Harper, my mum will be at Nightingale Lodge in three and a half hours! How do we get there? What do we do about the huskies? How will we fetch our stuff?"

"We have a confession too," Harper told the thieves of the Clue Club. "We stole these huskies from a cabin that didn't belong to us, which we've unintentionally wrecked."

"We might need your help," added Kat.

They had to tell their own story then. It was a relief to confess it to these strangers, who had somehow become friends and who listened without judging them. However, even they were shocked when Harper got to the part where Officer Burt Skinner seized her arm in the kitchen of the cabin and demanded to know where Riley was.

"Oh, what a tangled web we've woven," rued Cath. "Dare I ask if Officer Skinner could have followed you?"

Kat assured her that he definitely hadn't and made everyone laugh with her description of the crooked policeman going down in a whirl of arms, legs, and whipped-up snow after Thunder disobeyed orders and nipped him.

"Last we saw, he was lying on his roly-poly tummy like a dung beetle. I suspect that as soon as he managed to get up again, he'll have headed for the hills—or the hospital—to get his raccoon and dog bites checked out. The doctor will probably recommend tetanus and rabies shots. Those are painful. I doubt he'll be thinking about diamonds or Riley for a day or two at least."

"Couldn't have happened to a nicer man," said Bianca.

Everyone smiled except Kat and Harper, who were worrying once more about how to return the huskies and get to Nightingale Lodge.

Georgia giggled. "Don't look so dejected, girls. You're talking to people with real problems. Yours are nothing. I've just noticed that my phone finally has a signal. We'll start by calling Riley's dad. It might be best if only Cath is here with her when he arrives. Sounds as if they have family business to take care of."

"Agreed," said Cath.

"Meantime, Kiara and Rob will drive you and Harper to Nightingale Lodge. Michael, me, Bianca, and Emilio will return the huskies to the kennels at the Dog House and divide up the chores. Some of us will clean, others can dash to the grocery and housewares store to pick up replacements for the food and cushions or whatever."

She grinned. "Start by writing a wish list of things you'd put back in the Dog House if you could."

The girls were overwhelmed.

"I don't know how to thank you," said Kat.

"Don't mention it. One good turn deserves another."

ICE IS NICE

"HARPER, ARE YOU SURE YOU WOULDN'T prefer to go ice-skating at Rockefeller Center or tobogganing in Central Park?" asked Professor Lamb. "It'd be no trouble. I know how much you love hurtling down a slope of new-fallen snow."

"Not today, thanks, Dad," said Harper with a shudder. "Maybe not ever."

"Not ever! I thought—"

"What Harper means," Kat cut in hastily, "is that as fun as it's been to enjoy the great outdoors, we're keen to see the other side of New York. The *indoor* side."

"That's understandable," sympathized her mum. "You've experienced enough snow to last a lifetime. But if it's an indoor attraction you're in the mood for, we could visit the iconic Metropolitan Museum, the Empire State Building, the Top of the Rock Observation Deck, or even take in a show on Broadway. Why were you both so insistent that we come here, to the scene of a diamond heist?"

"The same question crossed my mind," said Theo Lamb as they climbed out of the limousine. A bellman in a black frock coat with gold buttons and snazzy red trim rushed to usher them into the Royal Manhattan. "And why are you being so mysterious about it? What's the big secret?"

A relay of suited and booted staff directed them to the grand salon via a maze of corridors adorned with royal-blue carpets and gilt-edged oil paintings of smug aristocrats.

"Kat says we have to be patient," Ellen Wolfe told the professor. "All will be revealed after we've had tea. I've been laughing ever since she said it. It put me in mind of Hercule Poirot asking guests to assemble in the dining car of the train before he unveiled the killer. Or were there several killers? It's so long since I've read *Murder on the Orient Express*."

"Mum!" Kat was embarrassed.

An amused and slightly bored waiter escorted them to their table.

"Our daughters are obsessed with the heist that happened here," Dr. Wolfe told him as he filled their water glasses and shook out the starched napkins with a professional flick.

"Your daughters and hundreds of others." The waiter smiled. "Thanks to Hollywood, I guess there is a dark glamour to the theft of millions of dollars' worth of diamonds. The necklace has never been recovered, you know. I think some people come here secretly hoping to find it. The grand salon is booked solid for months."

"Is it?" Dr. Wolfe looked quizzically at Kat. "But Wainwright Matthews contacted us just yesterday to kindly offer us tea. I wonder how he got a reservation."

The waiter cocked an ear. "The chairman of Daylesford Bank? We host all of his bank's conferences and special events. Mr. Matthews can get a table any day of the year. As you may have heard, his daughter witnessed the stealing of the diamonds."

He smiled. "Ma'am, name's Remy. I'd be glad to show the girls the ballroom where the heist took place—if that's all right with you."

"We'd love that!" answered Harper.

"Not before we've ordered our tea," instructed her father.

Remy listed the day's specials and promised to return shortly for their order.

Dr. Wolfe gave Kat a considering glance. "Who could have predicted that the cat photo you gave a lonely girl on our first day in the Adirondacks might help save her life? It shows the importance of kindness to strangers. Even so, it's extremely generous of Riley's father to thank you by sending his limousine all the way to the Adirondacks to drive us in for afternoon tea at the Royal Manhattan. What a treat."

"What I'd like to know is how Mr. Wainwright tracked us down when Kat never gave Riley her details," remarked the professor.

"Dad, nowadays it's possible to find almost anyone, anywhere, with a few taps of a keyboard," said his daughter without thinking, prompting a row about the dangers of the internet.

Thankfully, the waiter reappeared before Professor Lamb could get into his stride.

"Remy, would now be convenient for you to show us the ballroom?" Harper asked sweetly.

In Kat's imagination, the ballroom scene had always been suspended in time. She half expected it to be that way in real life too.

When Remy pushed open the double doors, it wouldn't have surprised her if a jazz band was playing as it had on the night of the launch the east wing. Politicians and celebrities would be clinking champagne glasses and nibbling canapés from silver trays as they moved between glittering ice sculptures and fiberglass icebergs.

Today, the empty, stale-smelling ballroom was being readied for a less glamorous audience. A crooked sign welcomed the American Association of Wellness Regulators.

"That's all there is to see," said Remy, ready to leave. "Nothing exciting."

Harper stayed where she was. "What's puzzling is how the supposed thief, Gerry Meeks, got an invitation to the event. He wasn't rich or famous."

Remy grimaced. "My girlfriend almost lost her job over that. She was one of the meet-and-greeters that evening. She spotted Mr. Meeks wandering about like a stray lamb and asked for his name so she could assist him to his table. It wasn't on the guest list, but he was in a tuxedo, looking as if he was meant to be there. She assumed there'd been a mistake. He was so wobbly she was also a bit worried he might collapse. She helped him to a spare seat at the table behind Cynthia Hollinghurst and her friends. The rest is history."

"We heard it was an arctic-themed event," said Kat. "Was there a lot of ice?"

"Was there ever. We could have donated it to the Bronx Zoo and made a playground for ten thousand penguins. The ice truck came and went on the hour. The back-room staff nearly got frostbite dealing with it. We had crushed ice, sliced ice, ice cubes, dry ice, and iced polar bears. Cryogenic chocolate honeycomb ice cream too. We were having to get creative about where to keep it all."

"What happened to it at the end of the night?"

He laughed. "It melted and went down the drain. What do you think happened? There are strict rules around the storage of ice. Health and safety and so on. Our ice storage bins are emptied and refilled every time the iceman comes."

"That's annoying," said Harper, as crushed as the ice that had slipped down the drain.

"Excuse me?"

"I said, that must be boring. All the emptying and refilling. Waste of water too." Harper forced a smile. She and Kat had come up with an elaborate theory about the fate of the missing diamond necklace while hiking through the melting snow and ice left by Storm Mindy. They'd been dying to test it out. Once again, they were too late.

Remy's phone buzzed in his pocket. "Gotta run. Can you girls find your way back to the grand salon on your own?"

Kat and Harper bit their tongues. If they could survive bear attacks and navigate three frozen rivers with six huskies, they were fairly sure they could make it along two carpeted corridors.

"We'll manage," Harper assured him.

After he'd gone, she said despondently, "That's the problem with solving mysteries on paper. It doesn't always work in real life. I'm clean out of ideas. How about you?"

Kat didn't answer. She walked into the center of the ballroom, trying to picture the scene. "Let's go over it one last time. Riley says the reason she noticed Gerry is because he tripped and jostled Cynthia's friend, who then bumped into Cynthia. Doesn't matter if it was an accident or if he did it deliberately while trying to steal the necklace. What matters is that while Cynthia recovered and started posing for photos, Riley saw him stuff the diamonds in his pocket."

Harper joined her on the ballroom floor. "According to Riley, when Gerry realized he'd been caught red-handed—by a twelve-year-old—he was shame-faced. In pretty much the same moment, Cynthia discovers her necklace has gone and starts screaming the place down. In the chaos, Riley loses sight of Gerry. If you were him, what would you do next?"

"I'd get rid of the diamonds," said Kat. "Pretend I'd never wanted to steal them in the first place."

"How?"

"He could have given them back to Cynthia, made out he'd found them on the floor?"

"That was the easy solution," said Harper, "but it may not have been possible."

"Why not?"

"Gerry's ninety-one and unsteady on his feet. Our theory was that the diamonds were either knocked from his grasp as people crowded around Cynthia or he flung them away in a panic. If they'd landed on the floor, there's a good chance they'd have been given back to Cynthia. If they landed on the tray of canapés on ice that was going by in the photo we saw, they would have been invisible among the crushed ice. Cynthia's diamonds would have ended their lives hanging out with the rats and potato peelings in a sewer somewhere."

"I really hoped that the necklace had landed in that cart going past to refill the ice machine," said Harper, "but Remy's blown that theory to bits."

"Excuse me," called a waitress from the door. "Are you Kat and Harper? Your parents asked me to let you know that tea has been served."

Crestfallen, they followed her back to the grand salon. They'd been so certain they were right that failure had never been an option.

As they walked into the grand salon, Kat heard a faint hum coming from behind a screen. Harper picked up on it too.

"What's behind there?" she asked the waitress.

"Oh, that. Some wallpaper was damaged by a clumsy staff member on the night the east wing was opened. It's hand-painted and we've been waiting for the artist to repair it for weeks."

"No, I mean, what's that humming sound?"

"A spare ice machine," said the waitress. "It's out of order because we haven't had a chance to empty it."

"I'll catch up," said Harper. "I just have to tie my shoelaces."

Twenty seconds later, she was sliding into her chair at the table.

"What now?" whispered Kat when she had a chance.

"Now we wait."

Between courses, Kat added extra ice to her pink lemonade.

"Are you ill, Kat?" asked her mother. "You've always loathed ice in your drinks."

"I've changed my mind. Ice is nice."

Their attention was diverted by a Pomeranian at the next table. It had a velvet collar.

"I really hope that its owner is not going to feed it a cream puff," said her mum. "Oh, I spoke too soon. She's just fed it a cream puff."

The dog reminded Kat of the huskies. In the limousine that morning, she and Harper had heard a radio interview with Torvill Andersen, the widow who owned the dogs. She'd been rushed to the hospital with a suspected burst appendix on the same afternoon that the girls had arrived in the Adirondacks.

Torvill lived alone, and it was days before anyone knew that she'd never made it back to the cabin. Nobody knew that the huskies had been left alone.

"As long as I live, I'll never forget the sight that greeted me when I returned to the cabin five and a half days later," a tearful Torvill told the reporter. "I feared that they'd have perished from hunger, thirst, and cold. Instead, they were in the best shape of their lives. Shiny, healthy, and content. My pet raccoon was missing, but then he always did have a mind of his own. The real shock, though, was the cabin."

"How so?"

"It was immaculate, even by my exacting standards, yet a great many things had been replaced. There were different cushions, new mugs and plates. My husky cookie jar had been replaced by one with a meerkat! A Raspberry Pi kit computer left sealed in a box had been professionally assembled. The morning I left, I made a three-bean chili and left it in the refrigerator—not knowing that it would be nearly a week before I returned. I thought I'd find it moldy. Instead, it had been replaced with a delicious fresh lasagna."

The reporter chuckled. "It's almost as if the three bears from the fairy tale moved into your cabin, ate your chili, slept in your bed, and exercised your huskies."

Torvill laughed too. "If those three bears are listening, I'd like to say you're welcome to stay anytime. Thank you, thank you, thank you for taking care of my babies."

"The Wrong Writers must have done a spectacular job of cleaning, cooking, and decorating the cabin," Kat whispered to Harper when her mum and the professor were distracted talking to the driver.

Harper giggled. "Would you expect anything less?"

The other interesting snippet of news on the five-hour journey to New York City was that the rogue state trooper who'd terrorized Harper had been charged with impersonating a park ranger and ambushing Riley's bodyguards' vehicle. It turned out that he owed a lot of money to some bad people. After eavesdropping on a police station conversation that revealed both Riley's identity and the location of the safe house, he became convinced that kidnapping her would solve his problems. Either she'd tell him where the diamond necklace was stashed, or he could pretend to rescue her and claim the ransom money that was offered by her banker father.

Kat suddenly became aware that her mum was speaking to her.

"Would you like me to invite Riley and her dad to stay with us in Bluebell Bay next spring or summer? On TV this morning, he said that coming so close to losing Riley had helped remind him that love means more than money."

Kat had gotten the same impression. "I'm not a nature person like Riley," Wainwright Matthews had said. "I'm a city person through and through. But my daughter has promised to teach me some wilderness stuff. She built a snow shelter to survive, you know. We're going to try camping. And before you ask, yes, we're getting a kitten."

Before Kat could answer her mum, a commotion

erupted near the Japanese silk screen. A manager in a designer suit was pointing a polished red fingernail at a puddle and lecturing a waiter with increasing volume.

"Eddie . . . idiotic . . . Guests could SLIP . . . Break an arm! Do you have any idea what a DISASTER . . . No excuses . . . RECORD-BREAKING LAWSUIT!"

Harper stood up. "Ma'am, Eddie didn't unplug the ice machine. I did."

Kat stood too. "I helped."

Dr. Wolfe let out a little shriek. "Kat! Harper! Why would you do such a terrible thing?"

Professor Lamb's chair overturned with a crash. "Ma'am, I'm so sorry. My daughter isn't usually so discourteous or thoughtless. I don't know what's come over her."

The manager forced an ingratiating smile. "You heard the gentleman, folks," she told the intrigued and gawking tearoom guests. "A minor misunderstanding. Kids will be kids. Please accept my sincere apologies. Enjoy the rest of your afternoon."

She strode across to the Wolfes and Lambs' table on no-nonsense heels. "Thanks for your honesty, girls. However, I must ask you all to leave. Our guests expect peace and luxury when they come to the Royal Manhattan."

"We're guests of Wainwright Matthews, whose daughter, Riley, witnessed the theft of the diamonds," said Harper, ignoring her father's warning hand on her arm. "Aren't you going to ask us why we did what we did?"

The manager's stare was colder than a polar bear's toes. "You did something silly. No biggie. Wainwright Matthews is a valued customer of ours, and we'll say no more about it. We'll waive the check. Now I'd appreciate it if you'll leave quickly and quietly before I call security."

"What we did wasn't silly," Harper burst out, jumping to her feet. "We did it for the most important reason of all. To prove that the man accused of stealing the diamond necklace is innocent."

"Innocent?" cried a woman at a nearby table.

"This is ridiculous," said the manager. "You're ruining people's tea. Of course Mr. Meeks is not innocent. There was a witness. It was captured on CCTV."

"Yes, but the diamond necklace is still missing," said Kat, standing beside Harper and ignoring her mum's attempts to tug her down. "What if we could prove that the necklace never left the hotel in the first place? What if this is all a terrible 'misunderstanding,' as you call it?"

"This is better than Miss Marple," said a man at the next table, beaming. "If these diamonds never left the hotel, where are they now?"

"In the ice machine behind the screen," said Harper.

The crowd gasped. Nobody cared about tranquil teas now.

"If what we're saying really *is* ridiculous, then you have nothing to lose by letting us have a look," said Harper. "The worst that can happen is that the diamonds are not there and Kat and I look like fools. The best that can happen is that you get promoted because the Royal Manhattan is saved from paying out millions to Mr. Hollinghurst."

"Fine, let's get it over with," snapped the manager. "But if you're wrong, I'm calling down the general manager. Somebody is going to have to compensate the other guests for their destroyed afternoon tea."

She barked at their waiter, "Remy, you seem to be at loose ends. You go fishing in the ice machine."

The screen was moved aside without ceremony. Remy rolled up his sleeves and leaned over the ice machine. He swished around in the chilly soup of melting cubes. Then he swished some more.

An agitated hum broke out across the grand salon. Some people were shouting for him to try harder, while others were demanding their money back.

Remy straightened up. A hush fell across the room. As he faced the manager, he opened his fist. Across his palm, dripping, sparkling, and the cause of so much trouble, lay Cynthia Hollinghurst's diamond necklace.

WISHFUL THINKING

"I CAN'T BELIEVE WE'RE FLYING HOME tonight," said Kat, bouncing on the extravagantly comfy mattress of the Royal Manhattan's junior suite.

Following the discovery of the diamond necklace, the hotel manager had insisted on giving them a free night in the hotel's finest accommodation. Dr. Wolfe and Theo Lamb each had suites fit for a king and queen, and the girls were sharing.

Harper was standing at their thirty-third-story window, looking down at the kaleidoscope of neon theater signs and rainbow crowds on Broadway. "For me, it's flying home but also leaving home. I love Bluebell Bay, but my heart belongs to the U.S. of A."

Kat knew what she meant. *They say that once you've breathed the High Peaks' air and felt the ruby rain on your skin, you'll be changed forever*, the woman in the Inquiring

Minds bookshop had said. It was true. The moment the red maple leaves had brushed Kat's upturned cheeks on that first day in the forest, something inside her had done a seismic shift.

A little piece of her heart would always belong to the Adirondacks.

All the same, she was counting the hours until she was on her not quite so extravagantly comfy futon in her attic room in Bluebell Bay, with Tiny taking up a leopard's share of the bed.

The doorbell rang. Their breakfast tray and morning newspaper were delivered on a silver platter.

Wrapped in fluffy white robes, they laid out the *New York Times* on the coffee table. They read it between bites of croissant.

WISH LIST GANGSTERS WERE WISHFUL THINKING, SAYS ATTORNEY

Detectives have been accused of having overactive imaginations after two girls—one British, one American—solved the case of the heiress's missing diamond necklace using sleuthing skills learned from mystery novels.

For close to two years, Americans have been gripped by the daring exploits of the Wish List gang. A 1964 Bob Dylan guitar, a fifth-century bronze, a priceless eighteenth-century

Sofia Rossi masterpiece, and more, all snaffled with apparent ease while hapless cops ran around in circles.

Incredibly, it now appears that those heists may also have been the stuff of fantasy.

NYPD detectives claimed that the gang's run of luck ended when alleged leader Gerry Meeks, 91, snatched heiress Cynthia Hollinghurst's $50 million necklace at the Royal Manhattan's grand east wing opening on September 27.

Yesterday, in a twist worthy of a thriller, schoolgirls Kat Wolfe, 12, and Harper Lamb, 13, sensationally revealed the diamonds to an enthralled audience of afternoon tea guests at the Royal Manhattan. The jewels had been in a stainless-steel ice storage unit all along.

How did the girls know where to look?

"It seemed obvious," said Harper Lamb, the daughter of eminent Yale paleontologist Theo Lamb.

Both girls are based in Bluebell Bay, an idyllic cove on England's Jurassic Coast. They became firm friends through a shared love of mysteries and animals.

Wolfe elaborated. "After we watched a news report where Mr. Meeks was charged with stealing the diamond necklace and other crimes, we felt sorry for him. People seemed to be judging him before he was proven guilty. When Storm Mindy came along, and we were trapped in a snowy cabin in the Adirondacks with nothing to do, we decided to put our heads together and consider other options."

"We got lucky," Lamb added modestly.

It was the latest in a series of rapid developments in the case. Earlier this week, an anonymous tip-off led police to recover all eight stolen items on the Wish List. They were undamaged and have been reunited with their owners. Did pranksters take them, or were the real thieves now suffering pangs of conscience? We may never know.

There have been winners and losers galore in this intriguing case.

The biggest loser is Clancy Hollinghurst, who has been charged with insurance fraud amid allegations that he claimed millions for the theft of an almost identical diamond necklace 30 years ago.

In a further twist, it has emerged that Mr. Meeks was the lead insurance investigator on the case.

Walking free from prison, Mr. Meeks had

only one comment: "We're all human. Every one of us makes mistakes. The real test is what we do about it."

Of the many unanswered questions in the case, one stands out. How did Mr. Meeks's DNA end up on the wish list found in his pocket on the night the diamonds were stolen?

His attorney, Rachel Scott, had this to say: "This case has only ever been about the wishful thinking of detectives. As I explained from the very beginning, Mr. Meeks has allergies. Soon after discovering the wish list, he sneezed on it. If everybody got locked up for hay fever, we'd be in trouble."

To celebrate his freedom, Meeks plans to move to the Adirondacks to live with friends. He will not be returning to Shady Oaks Nursing Home.

Harper folded the newspaper and tossed it on top of her suitcase.

"Do you think we did the right thing? With the money?"

"Yes, and I'd do it again in a heartbeat," said Kat. "Why, are you having second thoughts?"

"No, and I never will. Far as I'm concerned, the million-dollar reward wasn't ours to take. If anyone deserved it, it was Gerry. He was fighting to right lots of wrongs. We only helped with one."

Kat's phone rang as she brushed her teeth. She smiled as she wiped her mouth on a towel. "Hi, Grandfather."

"Katarina, according to my diary, a mere nine days have passed since you messaged me to say that you had 'sort of an emergency.' In hindsight, it may have been a mistake to escort you and your friends to the airport in my helicopter so that you didn't miss your flight."

"It wasn't a mistake, Grandfather. You were a miracle worker. I'm not sure what we'd have done without you."

"Kat, why do most people go on holiday?"

"To rest and relax."

"Did *you* rest and relax?"

"I, uh . . . not exactly, but that was Storm Mindy's fault. She buried us under so much snow and ice that Mum got stuck in Lake Placid and Professor Lamb was delayed in London. Harper and I were fine, but we had a couple of scrapes coping on our own in the wilderness."

"By 'scrapes,' I assume you're referring to the part you played in the rescue of Riley Matthews, star witness to one of the most high-profile diamond heists in the United States? A little bird tells me that Riley credits you with helping to save her life in a snowstorm after an attempted kidnapping."

"That wasn't me," said Kat. "It was Tiny."

"Who's Tiny?"

"You know—my Savannah cat in Bluebell Bay. Riley and I crossed paths in a forest. I ended up giving her a photo of Tiny because I got the feeling she needed a friend. His spirit kept her going when she was lost in a blizzard."

"Your cat in Bluebell Bay kept her going?"

"It's a long story," said Kat.

"I'll bet it is. In the fullness of time, I'd be most interested to hear the details. And I suppose it's pure coincidence that you and Harper outsmarted some of America's finest detectives and just happened to know where to lay your hands on the missing necklace that caused all the trouble in the first place?"

"It was a lucky guess."

"So lucky that when you were offered a million-dollar reward, you promptly turned it down."

Kat didn't bother asking how her grandfather was so informed on matters that were known only to the people directly involved and would never see the light of day in any newspaper. Lord Hamilton-Crosse was always informed and always would be.

"We didn't turn down the reward. We asked for it to be donated—"

"To the new cancer wing of the St. Francis of Assisi Children's Hospital. Yes, I heard. I also heard that Gerry Meeks lost his young granddaughter to the cruel disease.

I can do the maths. But weren't you and Harper tempted by the thought of a college trust fund, or a million-dollar nest egg you could have spent on cars, clothes, or property once you came of age?"

"It wasn't our money to take," said Kat.

There was a long silence.

"Kat, I'm not sure where the truth in any of this lies," said her grandfather, "but what is beyond doubt is that, faced with a winter storm and a series of life-threatening challenges, you and Harper met all that they could throw at you with a courage and selflessness more rare, and infinitely more precious, than any diamonds owned by any heiress ever."

He seemed to have a frog in his throat and apologized for putting the call on hold while he blew his nose. "I hope you won't mind, Katarina," he said when he came back on the line, "but I've taken the liberty of donating an extra million dollars to the hospital fund on behalf of you and Harper."

Kat nearly dropped the phone. "You've what . . . I—I—"

She'd put the call on speakerphone. Harper had brought over a box of Kleenex because she was crying and laughing too.

"I don't know how to thank you, Grandfather."

"You can thank me by flying home safely tonight.

When you arrive at Heathrow tomorrow morning, my Spy Craft will be waiting to whisk you all home to Bluebell Bay. That way, you won't have to wait a moment longer than necessary to be reunited with Tiny. Sounds like he's a hero too—even if he doesn't know it."

TWO WRONGS AND
A RIGHT

THE GIRLS SPENT THEIR LAST DAY IN NEW
York City visiting the North and South Pools at the 9/11
Memorial and walking the High Line, an elevated park
where nature and art intermingled on a historic freight
railway line.

Kat was starving by the time they found a table at the
Buttercup Bake Shop on Broadway. But as she studied
the menu, the cake choices kept blurring. Ever since her
grandfather's call, she hadn't been able to stop thinking
about the unbreakable bond of hope, love, and reading
that had held the Wrong Writers together through so
many years and had, in the end, made the best of all
wishes come true.

"Mum, can I ask you a question?"

"Depends what it is," said Dr. Wolfe, inhaling
rapturously as a tray full of freshly baked chocolate

chip cookies sailed by. For the past hour, she'd seemed distracted, as if something had upset her. Kat had put it down to end-of-holiday blues, but now she wasn't so sure.

Her mum looked at her expectantly.

"Can two wrongs ever make a right?" asked Kat.

"No, darling, they can't. Well, except where cake and dessert are concerned. Ordering both the banana pudding and a red velvet cupcake might be wrong in some people's books, but it feels deliciously right."

"Mum, I'm serious."

"Are you asking if two wrongs and a right can ever be justified in a Robin Hood sense—by, say, taking from the rich to help the poor?"

"Exactly."

"No, it's still wrong. Morally, it's far better to put one's energy into volunteering for charities or picking up plastic rubbish on beaches or helping to rescue birds and animals. Real things that require real effort and care."

"But what if the wrongs involve stealing blood diamonds, like those in the necklace that me and Harper found, and the right involves saving sick children?"

"That," said her mum, "is a gray area."

Nothing further was said until they'd each eaten a banana pudding. Kat was making inroads into her hummingbird cupcake when Professor Lamb gave

Dr. Wolfe a meaningful look and they laid down their cake forks in unison.

Kat had an awful feeling that the moment of reckoning she and Harper had thus far avoided had arrived.

"Speaking of 'wrongs,'" Theo Lamb said heavily, "an hour ago, I received a text that shocked me to my core. Ross Ryan, who kindly lent us Nightingale Lodge, forwarded me a message from the caretaker, Mrs. Brody. She wished us a safe journey home and said what a pity it was that because of Storm Mindy, she'd never had a chance to meet any of us."

"*Any of us*," repeated Dr. Wolfe with quiet fury. "That includes you, Katarina Wolfe, and you, Harper Lamb."

"We debated whether to say anything," the professor continued, "but we didn't want to ruin your special day in New York City."

"Even though you've ruined ours," said Dr. Wolfe, glowering at the girls. "If I'd had the slightest inkling that while you were sending me chipper notes about apple crumbles and painting watercolors, you were alone in the wilderness in the midst of a deadly winter storm, I'd have had a nervous breakdown."

Theo Lamb, the most mild-mannered, easygoing man Kat had ever known, was apoplectic and struggling to keep his voice down. "How could you lie about Annette Brody taking care of you when you hadn't even met her?"

"We didn't lie," protested his daughter. "We'd never do that."

"You neglected to mention it, which is exactly the same thing."

"We didn't want to worry you," said Kat.

"Well, honey, you've worried us now—retrospectively," raged her mother, albeit in a stage whisper.

With much sighing and scraping of chairs, the family at the next table moved tables. Dr. Wolfe smiled apologetically, but they ignored her.

Professor Lamb resumed the lecture. "Just because you're famous in the *New York Times* doesn't mean you get a free pass on deceiving us. If either of you ever pull a stunt like this again, you'll be grounded until you're eighteen. We'd ground you now except . . ."

A smile twitched at the corner of his mouth. "Except that in our heart of hearts we realize that you did what you did with noble intentions and for the best of all reasons. We're bowled over by your bravery."

"And by your housekeeping skills," added Dr. Wolfe. "Nightingale Lodge was spotless. Given the usual state of your bedroom, Kat, I'd never have believed you capable of it."

"You should see Harper's," Professor Lamb told her. "Volcanoes are less destructive."

"It was almost . . ." Dr. Wolfe's brow wrinkled, as if a concerning thought had just struck her. "It was almost as if you'd never set foot in the place until shortly before we arrived. I remember thinking at the time that your sheets looked freshly pressed."

"The cabin was so cold; that's what I noticed," said the professor, giving his daughter a hard stare. "Many of your messages mentioned blazing fires, yet the grate was curiously free of soot and ash. How did you stay warm with snow banking up to the windows? I've since learned that there was a power outage too. You never mentioned that. How did you survive?"

"With the help of three-bean chili heated on the gas stove and long bubble baths," enthused Kat, wincing when Harper kicked her beneath the table.

Her mum frowned. "Nightingale Lodge doesn't have a bath."

"Didn't stop me dreaming about them," Kat said hurriedly.

"What Kat's trying to say is that we are very, very sorry that we didn't tell you that the caretaker had gone AWOL," Harper put in.

"Mortified," agreed Kat.

"However, once Storm Mindy had gone and the

four of us were together at Nightingale Lodge, we had a heavenly vacation, didn't we, Dad? Dr. Wolfe?"

Their parents unbent and admitted it had been the best holiday ever.

"Maybe Ross's car breaking down was a good thing, Mum," said Kat. "You seemed to be thoroughly enjoying yourself at the spa in Lake Placid."

"I wouldn't say *enjoying* . . ."

"What would you say?" asked Kat with a sly grin.

"Okay, I admit it. I loved every minute," Dr. Wolfe said huffily. "Does that make me a bad mother?"

"It definitely doesn't. Besides, now that you've rested, relaxed, and recharged, you'll have more energy to give me extra attention," teased Kat.

Her mum laughed. "Perhaps I should have spa days on my own more often."

"I feel sorry for Dad," said Harper. "While you were having pedicures and massages, Dr. Wolfe, and Kat and I were off having entertaining adventures in the wilderness, he was stuck doing nothing in a soulless airport hotel."

"Er, since we're being honest, I didn't exactly do nothing," confessed her father. "I took the opportunity to catch up with friends at the Natural History Museum in London and see a few art exhibitions."

"So it wasn't quite the vacation we planned, but

somehow it worked out magnificently," said Dr. Wolfe with a smile. "Although I'd be most interested to hear more about your entertaining adventures in the wilderness, Kat and Harper . . . No, on second thought, don't tell me. I have enough gray hairs already."

"There were times when it did start to feel as if we were starring in our own mystery novel," mused Harper. "And who wouldn't want to get lost in a book?"

Kat grinned. "Beats being lost in the woods."

AUTHOR'S NOTE

Long before I wrote *The White Giraffe,* my first children's book, I was a journalist for the *Sunday Times* in London. At that point I hadn't yet discovered the joy of writing mysteries for children, and I was quite sure that reporting on sports and music was the best job in the world.

Why? Well, for one thing it's a passport to meeting some of the most extraordinary people on earth. I don't mean famous people, although I've interviewed Dolly Parton, Sia, Tiger Woods, and other stars of music, film, and sports along the way.

Looking back, the people who made the deepest impression on me were often the unseen and unsung heroes. Men and women who risked their lives to save refugees of war or natural disasters. Conservationists working in remote and dangerous outposts to save pangolins, rhinos, leopards, and other vanishing species. The teachers and librarians who inspire hope and transform difficult lives.

Not all heroes wear capes.

Many of my favorite assignments were investigations. I loved hunting for clues, meeting secret sources, and combing archives for snippets and links. It was a bit like being a detective. Once, I was sent to interview a traitorous spy on the run. Another time, a "good" spy helped me investigate Russian "sleeper" agents for a *Sunday Times* story. What I learned from him inspired the first book in this series, *Kat Wolfe Investigates*.

Becoming a writer is no way to get rich quick, but it's an excellent way to see the world. I've swam with wild dolphins in Australia, rescued leopards and dolphins from Cyprus and Turkey with the Born Free Foundation, cruised in the Galapagos Islands, and researched mysteries in places as far flung as St. Petersburg, Russia, and Namibia in Africa.

Few things are as thrilling as an American road trip. For years, I spent every spring following the PGA Tour. Mostly, I travelled with Robinson Holloway, another young reporter, and mostly we stayed at seedy budget motels and ate at the Waffle House. Robinson is one of the smartest, funniest, kindest women I've ever known, and although we were mostly broke, we had so much fun cruising down the interstate listening to country music.

The minute I decided to set *Kat Wolfe on Thin Ice* in the Adirondacks, Robinson was the first person I called. Thankfully, she was free at short notice. We met in New Jersey, hopped into her car, turned on the country music, and hit the road.

I knew that I wanted part of the plot to unfold in New York City, which I adore. I also knew that I wanted the cabin in which Kat and Harper find themselves to be located in true wilderness. It was my editor, Wesley Adams, who suggested the Adirondacks.

It was a perfect fit. Robinson and I stayed with local scientists, Deb Roberts and Bob Singer. As well as being open-water swimmers, they've canoed practically every key lake and river in the six-million-acre park.

To begin with, I found the sheer size of the Adirondacks overwhelming. I couldn't imagine how I'd find the exact right place for Kat and Harper's cabin. But Bob, it turned out, had his own plane. He was also a superb pilot. He took me flying over the Adirondack mountains and there, on a blue lake surrounded by forest I saw the ideal spot.

Between Deb and Bob and the friendly locals we met in coffee shops, we were able to find the lesser-known trails at the height of the fall colors. The scenery was truly stunning. In one forest, I experienced what Riley does in my novel: ruby rain. The soft, jewel-like sound of the leaves falling will stay with me always.

The reason I go to such lengths to research my novels is in the hope that the reader will feel, *really feel,* that they're standing in the shoes of Kat and Harper and solving the mystery along with them.

In the short time since I traveled to the Adirondacks, Covid-19 has changed the world beyond recognition. Few places have been hit harder than New York City, and few inhabitants have fought back with such courage. Every day, in every way, ordinary heroes are rising to the challenge, saving lives, and bringing smiles to hospitals, care homes, and communities.

Wherever you live, hold fast to hope and kindness. Those are the things that'll see us all through. And if, like me, you love reading, you'll know this simple truth. There is no better escape than getting lost in a book.

Keep reading and follow your dreams.

Lauren St John, 2020

ACKNOWLEDGMENTS

Whenever I do school visits or speak at literary festivals, two questions almost always come up: "Where do you get your ideas?" and "How long does it take to write a book?"

In a way, they're different parts of the same question. For instance, the idea for *Kat Wolfe Takes the Case* was partly inspired by my childhood on a farm and game reserve in Zimbabwe, and the life-changing experiences I had rescuing dolphins and leopards with the Born Free Foundation.

Other things influenced the plot too. Research trips to the Jurassic Coast, a newspaper clipping on the fossil trade, and an encounter with rhinos at Shamwari Game Reserve. As for *Kat Wolfe on Thin Ice,* it might not have existed were it not for the many thousands of miles I drove with Robinson Holloway while covering the PGA Tour.

What I'm trying to say is, it's very hard to pinpoint where books begin because so many chance meetings and life experiences go into each and every character and detail. It's a bit like sowing a wildflower meadow. Sometimes you're surprised by what comes up!

Throughout the writing of this book, so many wonderful people have supported me, been endlessly patient with me, had spirit-restoring coffees or Zoom calls with me, made me laugh, and handed me boxes of Kleenex on the days when it all seemed impossible.

Huge thanks to Catherine Clarke at Felicity Bryan Associates, Venetia Gosling at Gosling Editorial, and Lucy Pearse at Macmillan Children's Books for doing pretty much all those things. It's been a joy.

Special thanks also brilliant Wesley Adams, my editor at Farrar, Straus and Giroux, not least for suggesting I set my snowy cabin mystery in the Adirondacks! Like Kat, I left a bit of my heart in the High Peaks forests. Both Daniel Deamo and Dung Ho have captured Kat and Harper, the huskies, and autumn in the Adirondacks perfectly.

At MCB in London, Jo Hardace, Amber Ivatt, Sarah Clarke, and Belinda Rasmussen are the best publishing team any author could hope to have. The same is true at FSG in New York. Thanks to Melissa Warten, Lelia Mander, Erica Ferguson, and Valerie Shea at FSG).

Of course, *Kat Wolfe on Thin Ice* would have been a very different book had Deb Roberts and Bob Singer not taken two virtual strangers under their wing in the Adirondacks. Thanks so much for the advice, map-reading, and hospitality, and to Bob particularly for the unforgettable flight over the Adirondacks. Robinson, thanks for leaving Ginger and Poki to organize one of our best-ever road trips. Until the next time ...

There are many good things about being a children's author, but one of my favorites is the community of children's authors. Thanks to Abi Elphinstone, Katherine Rundell, and Piers Torday for the spirit-lifting Zoom coffees. The next socially-distanced dinner is on me!

Thanks also to Emelia Sithole-Matarise and my godson, Matis, for the walks, talks, and daily inspiration, and my Mom, Dad, and sister, Lisa, for being there through thick and thin.

Last but not least, thanks to Merina McInnes for the room with the view of deer, kites, blue jays, foxes, voles, blue tits, goldfinches, and green parrots. It's made all the difference in the world.